M.E Brad

CW00547842

John Marchmon

Volume 3

M.E Braddon

John Marchmont's Legacy
Volume 3

1st Edition | ISBN: 978-3-75232-621-5

Place of Publication: Frankfurt am Main, Germany

Year of Publication: 2020

Outlook Verlag GmbH, Germany.

JOHN MARCHMONT'S LEGACY.

BY M.E. Braddon

VOL. III.

CHAPTER I.

Edward Arundel went back to his lonely home with a settled purpose in his mind. He would leave Lincolnshire,—and immediately. He had no motive for remaining. It may be, indeed, that he had a strong motive for going away from the neighbourhood of Lawford Grange. There was a lurking danger in the close vicinage of that pleasant, old-fashioned country mansion, and the bright band of blue-eyed damsels who inhabited there.

"I will turn my back upon Lincolnshire for ever," Edward Arundel said to himself once more, upon his way homeward through the October twilight; "but before I go, the whole country shall know what I think of Paul Marchmont."

He clenched his fists and ground his teeth involuntarily as he thought this.

It was quite dark when he let himself in at the old-fashioned half-glass door that led into his humble sitting-room at Kemberling Retreat. He looked round the little chamber, which had been furnished forty years before by the proprietor of the cottage, and had served for one tenant after another, until it seemed as if the spindle-legged chairs and tables had grown attenuated and shadowy by much service. He looked at the simple room, lighted by a bright fire and a pair of wax-candles in antique silver candlesticks. The red firelight flickered and trembled upon the painted roses on the walls, on the obsolete engravings in clumsy frames of imitation-ebony and tarnished gilt. A silver tea-service and a Sèvres china cup and saucer, which Mrs. Arundel had sent to the cottage for her son's use, stood upon the small oval table: and a brown setter, a favourite of the young man's, lay upon the hearth-rug, with his chin upon his outstretched paws, blinking at the blaze.

As Mr. Arundel lingered in the doorway, looking at these things, an image rose before him, as vivid and distinct as any apparition of Professor Pepper's manufacture; and he thought of what that commonplace cottage-chamber might have been if his young wife had lived. He could fancy her bending over the low silver teapot,—the sprawling inartistic teapot, that stood upon quaint knobs like gouty feet, and had been long ago banished from the Dangerfield breakfast-table as utterly rococo and ridiculous. He conjured up the dear dead face, with faint blushes flickering amidst its lily pallor, and soft hazel eyes looking up at him through the misty steam of the tea-table, innocent and virginal as the eyes of that mythic nymph who was wont to appear to the old Roman king. How happy she would have been! How willing to give up fortune and station, and to have lived for ever and ever in that queer old cottage, ministering to him and loving him!

Presently the face changed. The hazel-brown hair was suddenly lit up with a glitter of barbaric gold; the hazel eyes grew blue and bright; and the cheeks blushed rosy red. The young man frowned at this new and brighter vision; but he contemplated it gravely for some moments, and then breathed a long sigh, which was somehow or other expressive of relief.

"No," he said to himself, "I am *not* false to my poor lost girl; I do *not* forget her. Her image is dearer to me than any living creature. The mournful shadow of her face is more precious to me than the brightest reality."

He sat down in one of the spindle-legged arm-chairs, and poured out a cup of tea. He drank it slowly, brooding over the fire as he sipped the innocuous beverage, and did not deign to notice the caresses of the brown setter, who laid his cold wet nose in his master's hand, and performed a species of spirit-rapping upon the carpet with his tail.

After tea the young man rang the bell, which was answered by Mr. Morrison.

"Have I any clothes that I can hunt in, Morrison?" Mr. Arundel asked.

His factotum stared aghast at this question.

"You ain't a-goin' to 'unt, are you, Mr. Edward?" he inquired, anxiously.

"Never mind that. I asked you a question about my clothes, and I want a straightforward answer."

"But, Mr. Edward," remonstrated the old servant, "I don't mean no offence; and the 'orses is very tidy animals in their way; but if you're thinkin' of goin' across country,—and a pretty stiffish country too, as I've heard, in the way of bulfinches and timber,—neither of them 'orses has any more of a 'unter in him than I have."

"I know that as well as you do," Edward Arundel answered coolly; "but I am going to the meet at Marchmont Towers to-morrow morning, and I want you to look me out a decent suit of clothes—that's all. You can have Desperado saddled ready for me a little after eleven o'clock."

3

Mr. Morrison looked even more astonished than before. He knew his master's savage enmity towards Paul Marchmont; and yet that very master now deliberately talked of joining in an assembly which was to gather together for the special purpose of doing the same Paul Marchmont honour. However, as he afterwards remarked to the two fellow-servants with whom he sometimes condescended to be familiar, it wasn't his place to interfere or to ask any questions, and he had held his tongue accordingly.

Perhaps this respectful reticence was rather the result of prudence than of inclination; for there was a dangerous light in Edward Arundel's eyes upon this particular evening which Mr. Morrison never had observedbefore.

The factotum said something about this later in the evening.

"I do really think," he remarked, "that, what with that young 'ooman's death, and the solitood of this most dismal place, and the rainy weather,—which those as says it always rains in Lincolnshire ain't far out,—my poor young master is not the man he were."

He tapped his forehead ominously to give significance to his words, and sighed heavily over his supper-beer.

* * * * *

The sun shone upon Paul Marchmont on the morning of the 18th of October. The autumn sunshine streamed into his bedchamber, and awoke the new master of Marchmont Towers. He opened his eyes and looked about him. He raised himself amongst the down pillows, and contemplated the figures upon the tapestry in a drowsy reverie. He had been dreaming of his poverty, and had been disputing a poor-rate summons with an impertinent tax-collector in the dingy passage of the house in Charlotte Street, Fitzroy Square. Ah! that horrible house had so long been the only scene of his life, that it had grown almost a part of his mind, and haunted him perpetually in his sleep, like a nightmare of brick and mortar, now that he was rich, and had done with it for ever.

Mr. Marchmont gave a faint shudder, and shook off the influence of the bad dream. Then, propped up by the pillows, he amused himself by admiring his new bedchamber.

It was a handsome room, certainly—the very room for an artist and a sybarite. Mr. Marchmont had not chosen it without due consideration. It was situated in an angle of the house; and though its chief windows looked westward, being immediately above those of the western drawing-room, there was another casement, a great oriel window, facing the east, and admitting all the grandeur of the morning sun through painted glass, on which the Marchmont

4

escutcheon was represented in gorgeous hues of sapphire and ruby, emerald and topaz, amethyst and aqua-marine. Bright splashes of these colours flashed and sparkled on the polished oaken floor, and mixed themselves with the Oriental gaudiness of a Persian carpet, stretched beneath the low Arabian bed, which was hung with ruby-coloured draperies that trailed upon the ground. Paul Marchmont was fond of splendour, and meant to have as much of it as money could buy. There was a voluptuous pleasure in all this finery, which only a parvenu could feel; it was the sharpness of the contrast between the magnificence of the present and the shabby miseries of the past that gave a piquancy to the artist's enjoyment of his new habitation.

All the furniture and draperies of the chamber had been made by Paul Marchmont's direction; but its chief beauty was the tapestry that covered the walls, which had been worked, two hundred and fifty years before, by a patient chatelaine of the House of Marchmont. This tapestry lined the room on every side. The low door had been cut in it; so that a stranger going into that apartment at night, a little under the influence of the Marchmont cellars, and unable to register the topography of the chamber upon the tablet of his memory, might have been sorely puzzled to find an exit the next morning. Most tapestried chambers have a certain dismal grimness about them, which is more pleasant to the sightseer than to the constant inhabitant; but in this tapestry the colours were almost as bright and glowing to-day as when the fingers that had handled the variegated worsteds were still warm and flexible. The subjects, too, were of a more pleasant order than usual. No mailed ruffians or drapery-clad barbarians menaced the unoffending sleeper with uplifted clubs, or horrible bolts, in the very act of being launched from ponderous crossbows; no wicked-looking Saracens, with ferocious eyes and copper-coloured visages, brandished murderous scimitars above their turbaned heads. No; here all was pastoral gaiety and peaceful delight. Maidens, with flowing kirtles and crisped yellow hair, danced before great wagons loaded with golden wheat. Youths, in red and purple jerkins, frisked as they played the pipe and tabor. The Flemish horses dragging the heavy wain were hung with bells and garlands as for a rustic festival, and tossed their untrimmed manes into the air, and frisked and gamboled with their awkward legs, in ponderous imitation of the youths and maidens. Afar off, in the distance, wonderful villages, very queer as to perspective, but all a-bloom with gaudy flowers and quaint roofs of bright-red tiles, stood boldly out against a bluer sky than the most enthusiastic pre-Raphaelite of to-day would care to send to the Academy in Trafalgar Square.

Paul Marchmont smiled at the youths and maidens, the laden wagons, the revellers, and the impossible village. He was in a humour to be pleased with everything to-day. He looked at his dressing-table, which stood opposite to

5

him, in the deep oriel window. His valet—he had a valet now—had opened the great inlaid dressing-case, and the silver-gilt fittings reflected the crimson hues of the velvet lining, as if the gold had been flecked with blood. Glittering bottles of diamond-cut glass, that presented a thousand facets to the morning light, stood like crystal obelisks amid the litter of carved-ivory brushes and Sèvres boxes of pomatum; and one rare hothouse flower, white and fragile, peeped out of a slender crystal vase, against a background of dark shining leaves.

"It's better than Charlotte Street, Fitzroy Square," said Mr. Marchmont, throwing himself back amongst the pillows until such time as his valet should bring him a cup of strong tea to refresh and invigorate his nerves withal. "I remember the paper in my room: drab hexagons and yellow spots upon a brown ground. *So* pretty! And then the dressing-table: deal, gracefully designed; with a shallow drawer, in which my razors used to rattle like castanets when I tried to pull it open; a most delicious table, exquisitely painted in stripes, olive-green upon stone colour, picked out with the favourite brown. Oh, it was a most delightful life; but it's over, thank Providence; it's over!"

Mr. Paul Marchmont thanked Providence as devoutly as if he had been the most patient attendant upon the Divine pleasure, and had never for one moment dreamed of intruding his own impious handiwork amid the mysterious designs of Omnipotence.

The sun shone upon the new master of Marchmont Towers. This bright October morning was not the very best for hunting purposes; for there was a fresh breeze blowing from the north, and a blue unclouded sky. But it was most delightful weather for the breakfast, and the assembling on the lawn, and all the pleasant preliminaries of the day's sport. Mr. Paul Marchmont, who was a thorough-bred Cockney, troubled himself very little about the hunt as he basked in that morning light. He only thought that the sun was shining upon him, and that he had come at last—no matter by what crooked ways—to the realisation of his great day-dream, and that he was to be happy and prosperous for the rest of his life.

He drank his tea, and then got up and dressed himself. He wore the conventional "pink," the whitest buckskins, the most approved boots and tops; and he admired himself very much in the cheval glass when this toilet was complete. He had put on the dress for the gratification of his vanity, rather than from any serious intention of doing what he was about as incapable of doing, as he was of becoming a modern Rubens or a new Raphael. He would receive his friends in this costume, and ride to cover, and follow the hounds, perhaps,—a little way. At any rate, it was very delightful to him to play the country gentleman; and he had never felt so much a country gentleman as at this moment, when he contemplated himself from head to heel in his hunting costume.

At ten o'clock the guests began to assemble; the meet was not to take place until twelve, so that there might be plenty of time for the breakfast.

I don't think Paul Marchmont ever really knew what took place at that long table, at which he sat for the first time in the place of host and master. He was intoxicated from the first with the sense of triumph and delight in his new position; and he drank a great deal, for he drank unconsciously, emptying his glass every time it was filled, and never knowing who filled it, or what was put into it. By this means he took a very considerable quantity of various sparkling and effervescing wines; sometimes hock, sometimes Moselle, very often champagne, to say nothing of a steady undercurrent of unpronounceable German hocks and crusted Burgundies. But he was not drunk after the common fashion of mortals; he could not be upon this particular day. He was not stupid, or drowsy, or unsteady upon his legs; he was only preternaturally excited, looking at everything through a haze of dazzling light, as if all the gold of his newly-acquired fortune had been melted into the atmosphere.

He knew that the breakfast was a great success; that the long table was spread with every delicious comestible that the science of a first-rate cook, to say nothing of Fortnum and Mason, could devise; that the profusion of splendid silver, the costly china, the hothouse flowers, and the sunshine, made a confused mass of restless glitter and glowing colour that dazzled his eyes as he looked at it. He knew that everybody courted and flattered him, and that he was almost stifled by the overpowering sense of his own grandeur. Perhaps he felt this most when a certain county magnate, a baronet, member of Parliament, and great landowner, rose,—primed with champagne, and rather thicker of utterance than a man should be who means to be in at the death, by-and-by,—and took the opportunity of—hum—expressing, in a few words,— haw—the very great pleasure which he—aw, yes—and he thought he might venture to remark,—aw—everybody about him—ha—felt on this most— arrah, arrah—interesting—er—occasion; and said a great deal more, which took a very long time to say, but the gist of which was, that all these country gentlemen were so enraptured by the new addition to their circle, and so altogether delighted with Mr. Paul Marchmont, that they really were at a loss to understand how it was they had ever managed to endure existence without him.

And then there was a good deal of rather unnecessary but very enthusiastic thumping of the table, whereat the costly glass shivered, and the hothouse blossoms trembled, amidst the musical chinking of silver forks; while the foxhunters declared in chorus that the new owner of Marchmont Towers was a jolly good fellow, which—*i.e.*, the fact of his jollity—nobody could deny.

It was not a very fine demonstration, but it was a very hearty one. Moreover, these noisy foxhunters were all men of some standing in the county; and it is a proof of the artist's inherent snobbery that to him the husky voices of these half-drunken men were more delicious than the sweet soprano tones of an equal number of Pattis—penniless and obscure Pattis, that is to say— sounding his praises. He was lifted at last out of that poor artist-life, in which he had always been a groveller,—not so much for lack of talent as by reason of the smallness of his own soul,—into a new sphere, where everybody was rich and grand and prosperous, and where the pleasant pathways were upon the necks of prostrate slaves, in the shape of grooms and hirelings, respectful servants, and reverential tradespeople.

Yes, Paul Marchmont was more drunken than any of his guests; but his drunkenness was of a different kind to theirs. It was not the wine, but his own grandeur that intoxicated and besotted him.

These foxhunters might get the better of their drunkenness in half an hour or so; but his intoxication was likely to last for a very long time, unless he should receive some sudden shock, powerful enough to sober him.

Meanwhile the hounds were yelping and baying upon the lawn, and the huntsmen and whippers-in were running backwards and forwards from the lawn to the servants' hall, devouring snacks of beef and ham,—a pound and a quarter or so at one sitting; or crunching the bones of a frivolous young chicken,—there were not half a dozen mouthfuls on such insignificant half-grown fowls; or excavating under the roof of a great game-pie; or drinking a quart or so of strong ale, or half a tumbler of raw brandy, *en passant*; and doing a great deal more in the same way, merely to beguile the time until the gentlefolks should appear upon the broad stone terrace.

It was half-past twelve o'clock, and Mr. Marchmont's guests were still drinking and speechifying. They had been on the point of making a move ever so many times; but it had happened every time that some gentleman, who had been very quiet until that moment, suddenly got upon his legs, and began to make swallowing and gasping noises, and to wipe his lips with a napkin; whereby it was understood that he was going to propose somebody's health. This had considerably lengthened the entertainment, and it seemed rather likely that the ostensible business of the day would be forgotten altogether. But at half-past twelve, the county magnate, who had bidden Paul Marchmont a stately welcome to Lincolnshire, remembered that there were twenty couple of impatient hounds scratching up the turf in front of the long windows of the banquet-chamber, while as many eager young tenant-farmers, stalwart yeomen, well-to-do butchers, and a herd of tag-rag and bobtail, were pining for the sport to begin;—at last, I say, Sir Lionel Boport remembered this, and led the way to the terrace, leaving the renegades to repose on the comfortable sofas lurking here and there in the spacious rooms. Then the grim stone front of the house was suddenly lighted up into splendour. The long terrace was one blaze of "pink," relieved here and there by patches of sober black and forester's green. Amongst all these stalwart, florid-visaged country gentlemen, Paul Marchmont, very elegant, very picturesque, but extremely unsportsmanlike, the hero of the hour, walked slowly down the broad stone steps amidst the vociferous cheering of the crowd, the snapping and yelping of impatient hounds, and the distant braying of a horn.

It was the crowning moment of his life; the moment he had dreamed of again and again in the wretched days of poverty and obscurity. The scene was scarcely new to him,—he had acted it so often in his imagination; he had heard the shouts and seen the respectful crowd. There was a little difference in detail; that was all. There was no disappointment, no shortcoming in the realisation; as there so often is when our brightest dreams are fulfilled, and the one great good, the all-desired, is granted to us. No; the prize was his, and it was worth all that he had sacrificed to win it.

He looked up, and saw his mother and his sisters in the great window over the porch. He could see the exultant pride in his mother's pale face; and the one redeeming sentiment of his nature, his love for the womankind who depended upon him, stirred faintly in his breast, amid the tumult of gratified ambition and selfish joy.

This one drop of unselfish pleasure filled the cup to the brim. He took off his hat and waved it high up above his head in answer to the shouting of the crowd. He had stopped halfway down the flight of steps to bow his acknowledgment of the cheering. He waved his hat, and the huzzas grew still louder; and a band upon the other side of the lawn played that familiar and triumphant march which is supposed to apply to every living hero, from a Wellington just come home from Waterloo, to the winner of a boat-race, or a patent-starch proprietor newly elected by an admiring constituency.

There was nothing wanting. I think that in that supreme moment Paul Marchmont quite forgot the tortuous and perilous ways by which he had reached this all-glorious goal. I don't suppose the young princes smothered in the Tower were ever more palpably present in Tyrant Richard's memory than when the murderous usurper grovelled in Bosworth's miry clay, and knew that the great game of life was lost. It was only when Henry the Eighth took away the Great Seal that Wolsey was able to see the foolishness of man's ambition. In that moment memory and conscience, never very wakeful in the breast of Paul Marchmont, were dead asleep, and only triumph and delight reigned in their stead. No; there was nothing wanting. This glory and grandeur paid him a thousandfold for his patience and self-abnegation during the past year.

He turned half round to look up at those eager watchers at the window.

Good God! It was his sister Lavinia's face he saw; no longer full of triumph and pleasure, but ghastly pale, and staring at someone or something horrible in the crowd. Paul Marchmont turned to look for this horrible something the sight of which had power to change his sister's face; and found himself confronted by a young man,—a young man whose eyes flamed like coals of fire, whose cheeks were as white as a sheet of paper, and whose firm lips were locked as tightly as if they had been chiseled out of a block of granite.

This man was Edward Arundel,—the young widower, the handsome soldier, —whom everybody remembered as the husband of poor lost Mary Marchmont.

He had sprung out from amidst the crowd only one moment before, and had dashed up the steps of the terrace before any one had time to think of hindering him or interfering with him. It seemed to Paul Marchmont as if his foe must have leaped out of the solid earth, so sudden and so unlooked-for was his coming. He stood upon the step immediately below the artist; but as the terrace-steps were shallow, and as he was taller by half a foot than Paul, the faces of the two men were level, and they confronted each other.

The soldier held a heavy hunting-whip in his hand—no foppish toy, with a golden trinket for its head, but a stout handle of stag-horn, and a formidable leathern thong. He held this whip in his strong right hand, with the thong twisted round the handle; and throwing out his left arm, nervous and muscular as the limb of a young gladiator, he seized Paul Marchmont by the collar of that fashionably-cut scarlet coat which the artist had so much admired in the cheval-glass that morning.

There was a shout of surprise and consternation from the gentlemen on the terrace and the crowd upon the lawn, a shrill scream from the women; and in the next moment Paul Marchmont was writhing under a shower of blows from the hunting-whip in Edward Arundel's hand. The artist was not physically brave, yet he was not such a cur as to submit unresistingly to this hideous disgrace; but the attack was so sudden and unexpected as to paralyse him—so rapid in its execution as to leave him no time for resistance. Before he had recovered his presence of mind; before he knew the meaning of Edward Arundel's appearance in that place; even before he could fully realise the mere fact of his being there,—the thing was done; he was disgraced for ever. He had sunk in that one moment from the very height of his new grandeur to the lowest depth of social degradation.

"Gentlemen!" Edward Arundel cried, in a loud voice, which was distinctly heard by every member of the gaping crowd, "when the law of the land suffers a scoundrel to prosper, honest men must take the law into their own hands. I wished you to know my opinion of the new master of Marchmont Towers; and I think I've expressed it pretty clearly. I know him to be a most consummate villain; and I give you fair warning that he is no fit associate for honourable men. Good morning."

Edward Arundel lifted his hat, bowed to the assembly, and then ran down the steps. Paul Marchmont, livid, and foaming at the mouth, rushed after him, brandishing his clenched fists, and gesticulating in impotent rage; but the young man's horse was waiting for him at a few paces from the terrace, in the care of a butcher's apprentice, and he was in the saddle before the artist could overtake him.

"I shall not leave Kemberling for a week, Mr. Marchmont," he called out; and then he walked his horse away, holding himself erect as a dart, and staring defiance at the crowd.

I am sorry to have to testify to the fickle nature of the British populace; but I am bound to own that a great many of the stalwart yeomen who had eaten game-pies and drunk strong liquors at Paul Marchmont's expense not half an hour before, were base enough to feel an involuntary admiration for Edward Arundel, as he rode slowly away, with his head up and his eyes flaming. There is seldom very much genuine sympathy for a man who has been horsewhipped; and there is a pretty universal inclination to believe that the man who inflicts chastisement upon him must be right in the main. It is true that the tenant-farmers, especially those whose leases were nearly run out, were very loud in their indignation against Mr. Arundel, and one adventurous spirit made a dash at the young man's bridle as he went by; but the general feeling was in favour of the conqueror, and there was a lack of heartiness even in the loudest expressions of sympathy.

The crowd made a lane for Paul Marchmont as he went back to the house, white and helpless, and sick with shame.

Several of the gentlemen upon the terrace came forward to shake hands with him, and to express their indignation, and to offer any friendly service that he might require of them by-and-by,—such as standing by to see him shot, if he should choose an old-fashioned mode of retaliation; or bearing witness against Edward Arundel in a law-court, if Mr. Marchmont preferred to take legal measures. But even these men recoiled when they felt the cold dampness of the artist's hands, and saw that *he had been frightened.* These sturdy, uproarious foxhunters, who braved the peril of sudden death every time they took a day's sport, entertained a sovereign contempt for a man who *could* be frightened of anybody or anything. They made no allowance for Paul Marchmont's Cockney education; they were not in the dark secrets of his life, and knew nothing of his guilty conscience; and it was *that* which had made him more helpless than a child in the fierce grasp of Edward Arundel.

So one by one, after this polite show of sympathy, the rich man's guests fell away from him; and the yelping hounds and the cantering horses left the lawn before Marchmont Towers; the sound of the brass band and the voices of the people died away in the distance; and the glory of the day was done.

Paul Marchmont crawled slowly back to that luxurious bedchamber which he had left only a few hours before, and, throwing himself at full length upon the bed, sobbed like a frightened child.

He was panic-stricken; not because of the horsewhipping, but because of a sentence that Edward Arundel had whispered close to his ear in the midst of the struggle.

"I know *everything*," the young man had said; "I know the secrets you hide in the pavilion by the river!"

CHAPTER II.

THE DESERTED CHAMBERS.

Edward Arundel kept his word. He waited for a week and upwards, but Paul Marchmont made no sign; and after having given him three days' grace over and above the promised time, the young man abandoned Kemberling Retreat, for ever, as he thought, and went away from Lincolnshire.

He had waited; hoping that Paul Marchmont would try to retaliate, and that some desperate struggle, physical or legal,—he scarcely cared which,—would occur between them. He would have courted any hazard which might have given him some chance of revenge. But nothing happened. He sent out Mr. Morrison to beat up information about the master of Marchmont Towers; and the factotum came back with the intelligence that Mr. Marchmont was ill, and would see no one—"leastways" excepting his mother and Mr. George Weston.

Edward Arundel shrugged his shoulders when he heard these tidings.

"What a contemptible cur the man is!" he thought. "There was a time when I could have suspected him of any foul play against my lost girl. I know him better now, and know that he is not even capable of a great crime. He was only strong enough to stab his victim in the dark, with lying paragraphs in newspapers, and dastardly hints and inuendoes."

It would have been only perhaps an act of ordinary politeness had Edward Arundel paid a farewell visit to his friends at the Grange. But he did not go near the hospitable old house. He contented himself with writing a cordial letter to Major Lawford, thanking him for his hospitality and kindness, and referring, vaguely enough, to the hope of a future meeting.

He despatched this letter by Mr. Morrison, who was in very high spirits at the prospect of leaving Kemberling, and who went about his work with almost boyish activity in the exuberance of his delight. The valet worked so briskly as to complete all necessary arrangements in a couple of days; and on the 29th of October, late in the afternoon, all was ready, and he had nothing to do but to superintend the departure of the two horses from the Kemberling railway-station, under the guardianship of the lad who had served as Edward's groom.

Throughout that last day Mr. Arundel wandered here and there about the house and garden that so soon were to be deserted. He was dreadfully at a loss what to do with himself, and, alas! it was not to-day only that he felt the burden of his hopeless idleness. He felt it always; a horrible load, not to be cast away from him. His life had been broken off short, as it were, by the catastrophe which had left him a widower before his honeymoon was well over. The story of his existence was abruptly broken asunder; all the better part of his life was taken away from him, and he did not know what to do with the blank and useless remnant. The ravelled threads of a once-harmonious web, suddenly wrenched in twain, presented a mass of inextricable confusion; and the young man's brain grew dizzy when he tried to draw them out, or to consider them separately.

His life was most miserable, most hopeless, by reason of its emptiness. He had no duty to perform, no task to achieve. That nature must be utterly selfish, entirely given over to sybarite rest and self-indulgence, which does not feel a lack of something wanting these,—a duty or a purpose. Better to be Sisyphus toiling up the mountain-side, than Sisyphus with the stone taken away from him, and no hope of ever reaching the top. I heard a man once—a bill-sticker, and not by any means a sentimental or philosophical person—declare that he had never known real prosperity until he had thirteen orphan grandchildren to support; and surely there was a universal moral in that bill-sticker's confession. He had been a drunkard before, perhaps,—he didn't say anything about that,—and a reprobate, it may be; but those thirteen small mouths clamoring for food made him sober and earnest, brave and true. He had a duty to do, and was happy in its performance. He was wanted in the world, and he was somebody. From Napoleon III., holding the destinies of civilised Europe in his hands, and debating whether he shall re-create Poland or build a new boulevard, to Paterfamilias in a Government office, working for the little ones at home,—and from Paterfamilias to the crossing-sweeper, who craves his diurnal halfpenny from busy citizens, tramping to their daily toil,—every man has his separate labour and his different responsibility. For ever and for ever the busy wheel of life turns round; but duty and ambition are the motive powers that keep it going.

Edward Arundel felt the barrenness of his life, now that he had taken the only revenge which was possible for him upon the man who had persecuted his wife. *That* had been a rapturous but brief enjoyment. It was over. He could do no more to the man; since there was no lower depth of humiliation—in these later days, when pillories and whipping-posts and stocks are exploded from our market-places—to which a degraded creature could descend. No; there was no more to be done. It was useless to stop in Lincolnshire. The sad suggestion of the little slipper found by the water-side was but too true. Paul Marchmont had not murdered his helpless cousin; he had only tortured her to death. He was quite safe from the law of the land, which, being of a positive and arbitrary nature, takes no cognisance of indefinable offences. This most infamous man was safe; and was free to enjoy his ill-gotten grandeur—if he could take much pleasure in it, after the scene upon the stone terrace.

The only joy that had been left for Edward Arundel after his retirement from the East India Company's service was this fierce delight of vengeance. He had drained the intoxicating cup to the dregs, and had been drunken at first in the sense of his triumph. But he was sober now; and he paced up and down the neglected garden beneath a chill October sky, crunching the fallen leaves under his feet, with his arms folded and his head bent, thinking of the barren future. It was all bare,—a blank stretch of desert land, with no city in the distance; no purple domes or airy minarets on the horizon. It was in the very nature of this young man to be a soldier; and he was nothing if not a soldier. He could never remember having had any other aspiration than that eager thirst for military glory. Before he knew the meaning of the word "war," in his very infancy, the sound of a trumpet or the sight of a waving banner, a glittering weapon, a sentinel's scarlet coat, had moved him to a kind of rapture. The unvarnished schoolroom records of Greek and Roman warfare had been as delightful to him as the finest passages of a Macaulay or a Froude, a Thiers or Lamartine. He was a soldier by the inspiration of Heaven, as all great soldiers are. He had never known any other ambition, or dreamed any other dream. Other lads had talked of the bar, and the senate, and *their* glories. Bah! how cold and tame they seemed! What was the glory of a parliamentary triumph, in which words were the only weapons wielded by the combatants, compared with a hand-to-hand struggle, ankle deep in the bloody mire of a crowded trench, or a cavalry charge, before which a phalanx of fierce Affghans fled like frightened sheep upon a moor! Edward Arundel was a soldier, like the Duke of Wellington or Sir Colin Campbell,—one writes the old romantic name involuntarily, because one loves it best,—or Othello. The Moor's first lamentation when he believes that Desdemona is false, and his life is broken, is that sublime farewell to all the glories of the battle-field. It was almost the same with Edward Arundel. The loss of his wife and of his captaincy were blent and mingled in his mind and he could only bewail the one great loss which left life most desolate.

He had never felt the full extent of his desolation until now; for heretofore he had been buoyed up by the hope of vengeance upon Paul Marchmont; and now that his solitary hope had been realised to the fullest possible extent, there was nothing left,—nothing but to revoke the sacrifice he had made, and to regain his place in the Indian army at any cost.

He tried not to think of the possibility of this. It seemed to him almost an infidelity towards his dead wife to dream of winning honours and distinction, now that she, who would have been so proud of any triumph won by him, was for ever lost.

So, under the grey October sky he paced up and down upon the grass-grown pathways, amidst the weeds and briars, the brambles and broken branches that crackled as he trod upon them; and late in the afternoon, when the day, which had been sunless and cold, was melting into dusky twilight, he opened the low wooden gateway and went out into the road. An impulse which he could not resist took him towards the river-bank and the wood behind Marchmont Towers. Once more, for the last time in his life perhaps, he went down to that lonely shore. He went to look at the bleak unlovely place which had been the scene of his betrothal.

It was not that he had any thought of meeting Olivia Marchmont; he had dismissed her from his mind ever since his last visit to the lonely boat-house. Whatever the mystery of her life might be, her secret lay at the bottom of a black depth which the impetuous soldier did not care to fathom. He did not want to discover that hideous secret. Tarnished honour, shame, falsehood, disgrace, lurked in the obscurity in which John Marchmont's widow had chosen to enshroud her life. Let them rest. It was not for him to drag away the curtain that sheltered his kinswoman from the world.

He had no thought, therefore, of prying into any secrets that might be hidden in the pavilion by the water. The fascination that lured him to the spot was the memory of the past. He could not go to Mary's grave; but he went, in as reverent a spirit as he would have gone thither, to the scene of his betrothal, to pay his farewell visit to the spot which had been for ever hallowed by the confession of her innocent love.

It was nearly dark when he got to the river-side. He went by a path which quite avoided the grounds about Marchmont Towers,—a narrow footpath, which served as a towing-path sometimes, when some black barge crawled by on its way out to the open sea. To-night the river was hidden by a mist,—a white fog,—that obscured land and water; and it was only by the sound of the horses' hoofs that Edward Arundel had warning to step aside, as a string of them went by, dragging a chain that grated on the pebbles by the river-side.

"Why should they say my darling committed suicide?" thought Edward Arundel, as he groped his way along the narrow pathway. "It was on such an evening as this that she ran away from home. What more likely than that she lost the track, and wandered into the river? Oh, my own poor lost one, God grant it was so! God grant it was by His will, and not your own desperate act, that you were lost to me!"

Sorrowful as the thought of his wife's death was to him, it soothed him to believe that death might have been accidental. There was all the difference betwixt sorrow and despair in the alternative.

Wandering ignorantly and helplessly through this autumnal fog, Edward Arundel found himself at the boat-house before he was aware of its vicinity.

There was a light gleaming from the broad north window of the painting-room, and a slanting line of light streamed out of the half-open door. In this lighted doorway Edward saw the figure of a girl,—an unkempt, red-headed girl, with a flat freckled face; a girl who wore a lavender-cotton pinafore and hob-nailed boots, with a good deal of brass about the leathern fronts, and a redundancy of rusty leathern boot-lace twisted round the ankles.

The young man remembered having seen this girl once in the village of Kemberling. She had been in Mrs. Weston's service as a drudge, and was supposed to have received her education in the Swampington union.

This young lady was supporting herself against the half-open door, with her arms a-kimbo, and her hands planted upon her hips, in humble imitation of the matrons whom she had been wont to see lounging at their cottage-doors in the high street of Kemberling, when the labours of the day were done.

Edward Arundel started at the sudden apparition of this damsel.

"Who are you, girl?" he asked; "and what brings you to this place?"

He trembled as he spoke. A sudden agitation had seized upon him, which he had no power to account for. It seemed as if Providence had brought him to this spot to-night, and had placed this ignorant country-girl in his way, for some special purpose. Whatever the secrets of this place might be, he was to know them, it appeared, since he had been led here, not by the promptings of curiosity, but only by a reverent love for a scene that was associated with his dead wife.

"Who are you, girl?" he asked again.

"Oi be Betsy Murrel, sir," the damsel answered; "some on 'em calls me 'Wuk-us Bet;' and I be coom here to cle-an oop a bit."

"To clean up what?"

"The paa-intin' room. There's a de-al o' moock aboot, and aw'm to fettle oop, and make all toidy agen t' squire gets well."

"Are you all alone here?"

"All alo-an? Oh, yes, sir."

"Have you been here long?"

The girl looked at Mr. Arundel with a cunning leer, which was one of her "wuk-us" acquirements.

"Aw've bin here off an' on ever since t' squire ke-ame," she said. "There's a deal o' cleanin' down 'ere."

Edward Arundel looked at her sternly; but there was nothing to be gathered from her stolid countenance after its agreeable leer had melted away. The young man might have scrutinised the figure-head of the black barge creeping slowly past upon the hidden river with quite as much chance of getting any information out of its play of feature.

He walked past the girl into Paul Marchmont's painting-room. Miss Betsy Murrel made no attempt to hinder him. She had spoken the truth as to the cleaning of the place, for the room smelt of soapsuds, and a pail and scrubbing-brush stood in the middle of the floor. The young man looked at the door behind which he had heard the crying of the child. It was ajar, and the stone-steps leading up to it were wet, bearing testimony to Betsy Murrel's industry.

Edward Arundel took the flaming tallow-candle from the table in the painting-room, and went up the steps into the pavilion. The girl followed, but she did not try to restrain him, or to interfere with him. She followed him with her mouth open, staring at him after the manner of her kind, and she looked the very image of rustic stupidity.

With the flaring candle shaded by his left hand, Edward Arundel examined the two chambers in the pavilion. There was very little to reward his scrutiny. The two small rooms were bare and cheerless. The repairs that had been executed had only gone so far as to make them tolerably inhabitable, and secure from wind and weather. The furniture was the same that Edward remembered having seen on his last visit to the Towers; for Mary had been fond of sitting in one of the little rooms, looking out at the slow river and the trembling rushes on the shore. There was no trace of recent occupation in the empty rooms, no ashes in the grates. The girl grinned maliciously as Mr. Arundel raised the light above his head, and looked about him. He walked in and out of the two rooms. He stared at the obsolete chairs, the rickety tables, the dilapidated damask curtains, flapping every now and then in the wind that rushed in through the crannies of the doors and windows. He looked here and there, like a man bewildered; much to the amusement of Miss Betsy Murrel, who, with her arms crossed, and her elbows in the palms of her moist hands, followed him backwards and forwards between the two small chambers.

"There was some one living here a week ago," he said; "some one who had the care of a——"

He stopped suddenly. If he had guessed rightly at the dark secret, it was better

18

that it should remain for ever hidden. This girl was perhaps more ignorant than himself. It was not for him to enlighten her.

"Do you know if anybody has lived here lately?" he asked.

Betsy Murrel shook her head.

"Nobody has lived here—not that *oi* knows of," she replied; "not to take their victuals, and such loike. Missus brings her work down sometimes, and sits in one of these here rooms, while Muster Poll does his pictur' paa-intin'; that's all *oi* knows of."

Edward went back to the painting-room, and set down his candle. The mystery of those empty chambers was no business of his. He began to think that his cousin Olivia was mad, and that her outbursts of terror and agitation had been only the raving of a mad woman, after all. There had been a great deal in her manner during the last year that had seemed like insanity. The presence of the child might have been purely accidental; and his cousin's wild vehemence only a paroxysm of insanity. He sighed as he left Miss Murrel to her scouring. The world seemed out of joint; and he, whose energetic nature fitted him for the straightening of crooked things, had no knowledge of the means by which it might be set right.

"Good-bye, lonely place," he said; "good-bye to the spot where my young wife first told me of her love."

He walked back to the cottage, where the bustle of packing and preparation was all over, and where Mr. Morrison was entertaining a select party of friends in the kitchen. Early the next morning Mr. Arundel and his servant left Lincolnshire; the key of Kemberling Retreat was given up to the landlord; and a wooden board, flapping above the dilapidated trellis-work of the porch, gave notice that the habitation was to be let.

CHAPTER III.

TAKING IT QUIETLY.

All the county, or at least all that part of the county within a certain radius of
Marchmont Towers, waited very anxiously for Mr. Paul Marchmont to make
some move. The horsewhipping business had given quite a pleasant zest, a
flavour of excitement, a dash of what it is the fashion nowadays to call
"sensation," to the wind-up of the hunting breakfast. Poor Paul's thrashing
had been more racy and appetising than the finest olives that ever grew, and
his late guests looked forward to a great deal more excitement and
"sensation" before the business was done with. Of course Paul Marchmont
would do something. He *must* make a stir; and the sooner he made it the
better. Matters would have to be explained. People expected to know the
cause of Edward Arundel's enmity; and of course the new master of the
Towers would see the propriety of setting himself right in the eyes of his
influential acquaintance, his tenantry, and retainers; especially if he
contemplated standing for Swampington at the next general election.

This was what people said to each other. The scene at the hunting-breakfast
was a most fertile topic of conversation. It was almost as good as a popular
murder, and furnished scandalous paragraphs *ad infinitum* for the provincial
papers, most of them beginning, "It is understood—," or "It has been
whispered in our hearing that—," or "Rochefoucault has observed that—."
Everybody expected that Paul Marchmont would write to the papers, and that
Edward Arundel would answer him in the papers; and that a brisk and stirring
warfare would be carried on in printer's-ink—at least. But no line written by
either of the gentlemen appeared in any one of the county journals; and by
slow degrees it dawned upon people that there was no further amusement to
be got out of Paul's chastisement, and that the master of the Towers meant to
take the thing quietly, and to swallow the horrible outrage, taking care to hide
any wry faces he made during that operation.

Yes; Paul Marchmont let the matter drop. The report was circulated that he
was very ill, and had suffered from a touch of brain-fever, which kept him a
victim to incessant delirium until after Mr. Arundel had left the county. This
rumour was set afloat by Mr. Weston the surgeon; and as he was the only
person admitted to his brother-in-law's apartment, it was impossible for any
one to contradict his assertion.

The fox-hunting squires shrugged their shoulders; and I am sorry to say that
the epithets, "hound," "cur," "sneak," and "mongrel," were more often

applied to Mr. Marchmont than was consistent with Christian feeling on the part of the gentlemen who uttered them. But a man who can swallow a sound thrashing, administered upon his own door-step, has to contend with the prejudices of society, and must take the consequences of being in advance of his age.

So, while his new neighbours talked about him, Paul Marchmont lay in his splendid chamber, with the frisking youths and maidens staring at him all day long, and simpering at him with their unchanging faces, until he grew sick at heart, and began to loathe all this new grandeur, which had so delighted him a little time ago. He no longer laughed at the recollection of shabby Charlotte Street. He dreamt one night that he was back again in the old bedroom, with the painted deal furniture, and the hideous paper on the walls, and that the Marchmont-Towers magnificence had been only a feverish vision; and he was glad to be back in that familiar place, and was sorry on awaking to find that Marchmont Towers was a splendid reality.

There was only one faint red streak upon his shoulders, for the thrashing had not been a brutal one. It was *disgrace* Edward Arundel had wanted to inflict, not physical pain, the commonplace punishment with which a man corrects his refractory horse. The lash of the hunting-whip had done very little damage to the artist's flesh; but it had slashed away his manhood, as the sickle sweeps the flowers amidst the corn.

He could never look up again. The thought of going out of this house for the first time, and the horror of confronting the altered faces of his neighbours, was as dreadful to him as the anticipation of that awful exit from the Debtor's Door, which is the last step but one into eternity, must be to the condemned criminal.

"I shall go abroad," he said to his mother, when he made his appearance in the western drawing-room, a week after Edward's departure. "I shall go on the Continent, mother; I have taken a dislike to this place, since that savage attacked me the other day."

Mrs. Marchmont sighed.

"It will seem hard to lose you, Paul, now that you are rich. You were so constant to us through all our poverty; and we might be so happy together now."

The artist was walking up and down the room, with his hands in the pockets of his braided velvet coat. He knew that in the conventional costume of a well-bred gentleman he showed to a disadvantage amongst other men; and he affected a picturesque and artistic style of dress, whose brighter hues and looser outlines lighted up his pale face, and gave a grace to his spare figure.

"You think it worth something, then, mother?" he said presently, half kneeling, half lounging in a deep-cushioned easy chair near the table at which his mother sat. "You think our money is worth something to us? All these chairs and tables, this great rambling house, the servants who wait upon us, and the carriages we ride in, are worth something, are they not? they make us happier, I suppose. I know I always thought such things made up the sum of happiness when I was poor. I have seen a hearse going away from a rich man's door, carrying his cherished wife, or his only son, perhaps; and I've thought, 'Ah, but he has forty thousand a year!' You are happier here than you were in Charlotte Street, eh, mother?"

Mrs. Marchmont was a Frenchwoman by birth, though she had lived so long in London as to become Anglicised. She only retained a slight accent of her native tongue, and a good deal more vivacity of look and gesture than is common to Englishwomen. Her elder daughter was sitting on the other side of the broad fireplace. She was only a quieter and older likeness of Lavinia Weston.

"*Am* I happier?" exclaimed Mrs. Marchmont. "Need you ask me the question, Paul? But it is not so much for myself as for your sake that I value all this grandeur."

She held out her long thin hand, which was covered with rings, some old-fashioned and comparatively valueless, others lately purchased by her devoted son, and very precious. The artist took the shrunken fingers in his own, and raised them to his lips.

"I'm very glad that I've made you happy, mother," he said; "that's something gained, at any rate."

He left the fireplace, and walked slowly up and down the room, stopping now and then to look out at the wintry sky, or the flat expanse of turf below it; but he was quite a different creature to that which he had been before his encounter with Edward Arundel. The chairs and tables palled upon him. The mossy velvet pile of the new carpets seemed to him like the swampy ground of a morass. The dark-green draperies of Genoa velvet deepened into black with the growing twilight, and seemed as if they had been fashioned out of palls.

What was it worth, this fine house, with the broad flat before it? Nothing, if he had lost the respect and consideration of his neighbours. He wanted to be a great man as well as a rich one. He wanted admiration and flattery, reverence and esteem; not from poor people, whose esteem and admiration were scarcely worth having, but from wealthy squires, his equals or his superiors by birth and fortune. He ground his teeth at the thought of his disgrace. He had drunk of the cup of triumph, and had tasted the very wine of life; and at the moment when that cup was fullest, it had been snatched away from him by the ruthless hand of his enemy.

Christmas came, and gave Paul Marchmont a good opportunity of playing the country gentleman of the olden time. What was the cost of a couple of bullocks, a few hogsheads of ale, and a waggon-load of coals, if by such a sacrifice the master of the Towers could secure for himself the admiration due to a public benefactor? Paul gave *carte blanche* to the old servants; and tents were erected on the lawn, and monstrous bonfires blazed briskly in the frosty air; while the populace, who would have accepted the bounties of a new Nero fresh from the burning of a modern Rome, drank to the health of their benefactor, and warmed themselves by the unlimited consumption of strong beer.

Mrs. Marchmont and her invalid daughter assisted Paul in his attempt to regain the popularity he had lost upon the steps of the western terrace. The two women distributed square miles of flannel and blanketing amongst greedy claimants; they gave scarlet cloaks and poke-bonnets to old women; they gave an insipid feast, upon temperance principles, to the children of the National Schools. And they had their reward; for people began to say that this Paul Marchmont was a very noble fellow, after all, by Jove, sir and that fellow Arundel must have been in the wrong, sir; and no doubt Marchmont had his own reasons for not resenting the outrage, sir; and a great deal more to the like effect.

After this roasting of the two bullocks the wind changed altogether. Mr. Marchmont gave a great dinner-party upon New-Year's Day. He sent out thirty invitations, and had only two refusals. So the long dining-room was filled with all the notabilities of the district, and Paul held his head up once more, and rejoiced in his own grandeur. After all, one horsewhipping cannot annihilate a man with a fine estate and eleven thousand a year, if he knows how to make a splash with his money.

Olivia Marchmont shared in none of the festivals that were held. Her father was very ill this winter; and she spent a good deal of her time at Swampington Rectory, sitting in Hubert Arundel's room, and reading to him. But her presence brought very little comfort to the sick man; for there was something in his daughter's manner that filled him with inexpressible terror; and he would lie for hours together watching her blank face, and wondering at its horrible rigidity. What was it? What was the dreadful secret which had transformed this woman? He tormented himself perpetually with this question, but he could imagine no answer to it. He did not know the power which a master-passion has upon these strong-minded women, whose minds are strong because of their narrowness, and who are the bonden slaves of one idea. He did not know that in a breast which holds no pure affection the master-fiend Passion rages like an all-devouring flame, perpetually consuming its victim. He did not know that in these violent and concentrative natures the line that separates reason from madness is so feeble a demarcation, that very few can perceive the hour in which it is passed.

Olivia Marchmont had never been the most lively or delightful of companions. The tenderness which is the common attribute of a woman's nature had not been given to her. She ought to have been a great man. Nature makes these mistakes now and then, and the victim expiates the error. Hence comes such imperfect histories as that of English Elizabeth and Swedish Christina. The fetters that had bound Olivia's narrow life had eaten into her very soul, and cankered there. If she could have been Edward Arundel's wife, she would have been the noblest and truest wife that ever merged her identity into that of another, and lived upon the refracted glory of her husband's triumphs. She would have been a Rachel Russell, a Mrs. Hutchinson, a Lady Nithisdale, a Madame de Lavalette. She would have been great by reason of her power of self-abnegation; and there would have been a strange charm in the aspect of this fierce nature attuned to harmonise with its master's soul, all the barbaric discords melting into melody, all the harsh combinations softening into perfect music; just as in Mr. Buckstone's most poetic drama we are bewitched by the wild huntress sitting at the feet of her lord, and admire her chiefly because we know that only that one man upon all the earth could have had power to tame her. To any one who had known Olivia's secret, there could have been no sadder spectacle than this of her decay. The mind and body decayed together, bound by a mysterious sympathy. All womanly roundness disappeared from the spare figure, and Mrs. Marchmont's black dresses hung about her in loose folds. Her long, dead, black hair was pushed away from her thin face, and twisted into a heavy knot at the back of her head. Every charm that she had ever possessed was gone. The oldest women generally retain some traits of their lost beauty, some faint reflection of the sun that has gone down, to light up the soft twilight of age, and even glimmer through the gloom of death. But this woman's face retained no token of the past. No empty hull, with shattered bulwarks crumbled by the fury of fierce seas, cast on a desert shore to rot and perish there, was ever more complete a wreck than she was. Upon her face and figure, in every look and gesture, in the tone of every word she spoke, there was an awful something, worse than the seal of death. Little by little the miserable truth dawned upon Hubert Arundel. His daughter was mad! He knew this; but he kept the dreadful knowledge hidden in his own breast,—a hideous secret, whose weight oppressed him like an actual burden. He kept the secret; for it would have seemed to him the most cruel treason against his daughter to have confessed his discovery to any living creature, unless it should be absolutely necessary to do so. Meanwhile he set himself to watch Olivia, detaining her at the Rectory for a week together, in order that he might see her in all moods, under all phases.

He found that there were no violent or outrageous evidences of this mental decay. The mind had given way under the perpetual pressure of one set of thoughts. Hubert Arundel, in his ignorance of his daughter's secrets, could not discover the cause of her decadence; but that cause was very simple. If the body is a wonderful and complex machine which must not be tampered with, surely that still more complex machine the mind must need careful treatment. If such and such a course of diet is fatal to the body's health, may not some thoughts be equally fatal to the health of the brain? may not a monotonous recurrence of the same ideas be above all injurious? If by reason of the peculiar nature of a man's labour, he uses one limb or one muscle more than the rest, strange bosses rise up to testify to that ill usage, the idle limbs wither, and the harmonious perfection of Nature gives place to deformity. So the brain, perpetually pressed upon, for ever strained to its utmost tension by the wearisome succession of thoughts, becomes crooked and one-sided, always leaning one way, continually tripping up the wretched thinker.

John Marchmont's widow had only one set of ideas. On every subject but that one which involved Edward Arundel and his fortunes her memory had decayed. She asked her father the same questions—commonplace questions relating to his own comfort, or to simple household matters, twenty times a day, always forgetting that he had answered her. She had that impatience as to the passage of time which is one of the most painful signs of madness. She looked at her watch ten times an hour, and would wander out into the cheerless garden, indifferent to the bitter weather, in order to look at the clock in the church-steeple, under the impression that her own watch, and her father's, and all the time-keepers in the house, were slow.

She was sometimes restless, taking up one occupation after another, to throw all aside with equal impatience, and sometimes immobile for hours together. But as she was never violent, never in any way unreasonable, Hubert Arundel had not the heart to call science to his aid, and to betray her secret. The thought that his daughter's malady might be cured never entered his mind as within the range of possibility. There was nothing to cure; no delusions to be exorcised by medical treatment; no violent vagaries to be held in check by drugs and nostrums. The powerful intellect had decayed; its force and clearness were gone. No drugs that ever grew upon this earth could restore that which was lost.

This was the conviction which kept the Rector silent. It would have given him unutterable anguish to have told his daughter's secret to any living being; but he would have endured that misery if she could have been benefitted thereby. He most firmly believed that she could not, and that her state was irremediable.

"My poor girl!" he thought to himself; "how proud I was of her ten years ago! I can do nothing for her; nothing except to love and cherish her, and hide her humiliation from the world."

But Hubert Arundel was not allowed to do even this much for the daughter he loved; for when Olivia had been with him a little more than a week, Paul Marchmont and his mother drove over to Swampington Rectory one morning and carried her away with them. The Rector then saw for the first time that his once strong-minded daughter was completely under the dominion of these two people, and that they knew the nature of her malady quite as well as he did. He resisted her return to the Towers; but his resistance was useless. She submitted herself willingly to her new friends, declaring that she was better in their house than anywhere else. So she went back to her old suite of apartments, and her old servant Barbara waited upon her; and she sat alone in dead John Marchmont's study, listening to the January winds shrieking in the quadrangle, the distant rooks calling to each other amongst the bare branches of the poplars, the banging of the doors in the corridor, and occasional gusts of laughter from the open door of the dining-room,—while Paul Marchmont and his guests gave a jovial welcome to the new year.

While the master of the Towers re-asserted his grandeur, and made stupendous efforts to regain the ground he had lost, Edward Arundel wandered far away in the depths of Brittany, travelling on foot, and making himself familiar with the simple peasants, who were ignorant of his troubles. He had sent Mr. Morrison down to Dangerfield with the greater part of his luggage; but he had not the heart to go back himself—yet awhile. He was afraid of his mother's sympathy, and he went away into the lonely Breton villages, to try and cure himself of his great grief, before he began life again as a soldier. It was useless for him to strive against his vocation. Nature had made him a soldier, and nothing else; and wherever there was a good cause to be fought for, his place was on the battle-field.

CHAPTER IV.

MISS LAWFORD SPEAKS HER MIND.

Major Lawford and his blue-eyed daughters were not amongst those guests who accepted Paul Marchmont's princely hospitalities. Belinda Lawford had never heard the story of Edward's lost bride as he himself could have told it; but she had heard an imperfect version of the sorrowful history from Letitia, and that young lady had informed her friend of Edward's animus against the new master of the Towers.

"The poor dear foolish boy will insist upon thinking that Mr. Marchmont was at the bottom of it all," she had said in a confidential chat with Belinda, "somehow or other; but whether he was, or whether he wasn't, I'm sure I can't say. But if one attempts to take Mr. Marchmont's part with Edward, he does get so violent and go on so, that one's obliged to say all sorts of dreadful things about Mary's cousin for the sake of peace. But really, when I saw him one day in Kemberling, with a black velvet shooting-coat, and his beautiful smooth white hair and auburn moustache, I thought him most interesting. And so would you, Belinda, if you weren't so wrapped up in that doleful brother of mine."

Whereupon, of course, Miss Lawford had been compelled to declare that she was not "wrapped up" in Edward, whatever state of feeling that obscure phrase might signify; and to express, by the vehemence of her denial, that, if anything, she rather detested Miss Arundel's brother. By-the-by, did you ever know a young lady who could understand the admiration aroused in the breast of other young ladies for that most uninteresting object, a *brother*? Or a gentleman who could enter with any warmth of sympathy into his friend's feelings respecting the auburn tresses or the Grecian nose of "a sister"? Belinda Lawford, I say, knew something of the story of Mary Arundel's death, and she implored her father to reject all hospitalities offered by Paul Marchmont.

"You won't go to the Towers, papa dear?" she said, with her hands clasped upon her father's arm, her cheeks kindling, and her eyes filling with tears as she spoke to him; "you won't go and sit at Paul Marchmont's table, and drink his wine, and shake hands with him? I know that he had something to do with Mary Arundel's death. He had indeed, papa. I don't mean anything that the world calls crime; I don't mean any act of open violence. But he was cruel to her, papa; he was cruel to her. He tortured her and tormented her until she—" The girl paused for a moment, and her voice faltered a little. "Oh, how I wish that I had known her, papa," she cried presently, "that I might have stood by her, and comforted her, all through that sad time!"

The Major looked down at his daughter with a tender smile,—a smile that was a little significant, perhaps, but full of love and admiration.

"You would have stood by Arundel's poor little wife, my dear?" he said. "You would stand by her *now*, if she were alive, and needed your friendship?"

"I would indeed, papa," Miss Lawford answered resolutely.

"I believe it, my dear; I believe it with all my heart. You are a good girl, my Linda; you are a noble girl. You are as good as a son to me, my dear."

Major Lawford was silent for a few moments, holding his daughter in his arms and pressing his lips upon her broad forehead.

"You are fit to be a soldier's daughter, my darling," he said, "or—or a soldier's wife."

He kissed her once more, and then left her, sighing thoughtfully as he went away.

This is how it was that neither Major Lawford nor any of his family were present at those splendid entertainments which Paul Marchmont gave to his new friends. Mr. Marchmont knew almost as well as the Lawfords themselves why they did not come, and the absence of them at his glittering board made his bread bitter to him and his wine tasteless. He wanted these people as much as the others,—more than the others, perhaps, for they had been Edward Arundel's friends; and he wanted them to turn their backs upon the young man, and join in the general outcry against his violence and brutality. The absence of Major Lawford at the lighted banquet-table tormented this modern rich man as the presence of Mordecai at the gate tormented Haman. It was not enough that all the others should come if these stayed away, and by their absence tacitly testified to their contempt for the master of the Towers.

He met Belinda sometimes on horseback with the old grey-headed groom behind her, a fearless young amazon, breasting the January winds, with her blue eyes sparkling, and her auburn hair blowing away from her candid face: he met her, and looked out at her from the luxurious barouche in which it was his pleasure to loll by his mother's side, half-buried amongst soft furry rugs and sleek leopard-skins, making the chilly atmosphere through which he rode odorous with the scent of perfumed hair, and smiling over cruelly delicious criticisms in newly-cut reviews. He looked out at this fearless girl whose friends so obstinately stood by Edward Arundel; and the cold contempt upon Miss Lawford's face cut him more keenly than the sharpest wind of that bitter January.

Then he took counsel with his womankind; not telling them his thoughts, fears, doubts, or wishes—it was not his habit to do that—but taking *their* ideas, and only telling them so much as it was necessary for them to know in order that they might be useful to him. Paul Marchmont's life was regulated by a few rules, so simple that a child might have learned them; indeed I regret to say that some children are very apt pupils in that school of philosophy to which the master of Marchmont Towers belonged, and cause astonishment to their elders by the precocity of their intelligence. Mr. Marchmont might have inscribed upon a very small scrap of parchment the moral maxims by which he regulated his dealings with mankind.

"Always conciliate," said this philosopher. "Never tell an unnecessary lie. Be agreeable and generous to those who serve you. N.B. No good carpenter would allow his tools to get rusty. Make yourself master of the opinions of others, but hold your own tongue. Seek to obtain the maximum of enjoyment with the minimum of risk."

Such golden saws as these did Mr. Marchmont make for his own especial guidance; and he hoped to pass smoothly onwards upon the railway of life, riding in a first-class carriage, on the greased wheels of a very easy conscience. As for any unfortunate fellow-travellers pitched out of the carriage-window in the course of the journey, or left lonely and helpless at desolate stations on the way, Providence, and not Mr. Marchmont, was responsible for *their* welfare. Paul had a high appreciation of Providence, and was fond of talking—very piously, as some people said; very impiously, as others secretly thought—about the inestimable Wisdom which governed all the affairs of this lower world. Nowhere, according to the artist, had the hand of Providence been more clearly visible than in this matter about Paul's poor little cousin Mary. If Providence had intended John Marchmont's daughter to be a happy bride, a happy wife, the prosperous mistress of that stately habitation, why all that sad business of old Mr. Arundel's sudden illness, Edward's hurried journey, the railway accident, and all the complications that had thereupon arisen? Nothing would have been easier than for Providence to have prevented all this; and then he, Paul, would have been still in Charlotte Street, Fitzroy Square, patiently waiting for a friendly lift upon the high-road of life. Nobody could say that he had ever been otherwise than patient. Nobody could say that he had ever intruded himself upon his rich cousins at the Towers, or had been heard to speculate upon his possible inheritance of the estate; or that he had, in short, done any thing but that which the best, truest, most conscientious and disinterested of mankind should do.

In the course of that bleak, frosty January, Mr. Marchmont sent his mother and his sister Lavinia to make a call at the Grange. The Grange people had never called upon Mrs. Marchmont; but Paul did not allow any flimsy ceremonial law to stand in his way when he had a purpose to achieve. So the ladies went to the Grange, and were politely received; for Miss Lawford and her mother were a great deal too innocent and noble-minded to imagine that these pale-faced, delicate-looking women could have had any part, either directly or indirectly, in that cruel treatment which had driven Edward's young wife from her home. Mrs. Marchmont and Mrs. Weston were kindly received, therefore; and in a little conversation with Belinda about birds, and dahlias, and worsted work, and the most innocent subjects imaginable, the wily Lavinia contrived to lead up to Miss Letitia Arundel, and thence, by the easiest conversational short-cut, to Edward and his lost wife. Mrs. Weston was obliged to bring her cambric handkerchief out of her muff when she talked about her cousin Mary; but she was a clever woman, and she had taken to heart Paul's pet maxim about the folly of *unnecessary* lies; and she was so candid as to entirely disarm Miss Lawford, who had a schoolgirlish notion that every kind of hypocrisy and falsehood was outwardly visible in a servile and slavish manner. She was not upon her guard against those practised adepts in the art of deception, who have learnt to make that subtle admixture of truth and falsehood which defies detection; like some fabrics in whose woof silk and cotton are so cunningly blended that only a practised eye can discover the inferior material.

So when Lavinia dried her eyes and put her handkerchief back in her muff, and said, betwixt laughing and crying,—

"Now you know, my dear Miss Lawford, you mustn't think that I would for a moment pretend to be sorry that my brother has come into this fortune. Of course any such pretence as that would be ridiculous, and quite useless into the bargain, as it isn't likely anybody would believe me. Paul is a dear, kind creature, the best of brothers, the most affectionate of sons, and deserves any good fortune that could fall to his lot; but I am truly sorry for that poor little girl. I am truly sorry, believe me, Miss Lawford; and I only regret that Mr. Weston and I did not come to Kemberling sooner, so that I might have been a friend to the poor little thing; for then, you know, I might have prevented that foolish runaway match, out of which almost all the poor child's troubles arose. Yes, Miss Lawford; I wish I had been able to befriend that unhappy child, although by my so doing Paul would have been kept out of the fortune he now enjoys—for some time, at any rate. I say for some time, because I do not believe that Mary Marchmont would have lived to be old, under the happiest circumstances. Her mother died very young; and her father, and her father's father, were consumptive."

Then Mrs. Weston took occasion, incidentally of course, to allude to her brother's goodness; but even then she was on her guard, and took care not to say too much.

"The worst actors are those who over-act their parts." That was another of Paul Marchmont's golden maxims.

"I don't know what my brother may be to the rest of the world," Lavinia said; "but I know how good he is to those who belong to him. I should be ashamed to tell you all he has done for Mr. Weston and me. He gave me this cashmere shawl at the beginning of the winter, and a set of sables fit for a duchess; though I told him they were not at all the thing for a village surgeon's wife, who keeps only one servant, and dusts her own best parlour."

And Mrs. Marchmont talked of her son; with no loud enthusiasm, but with a tone of quiet conviction that was worth any money to Paul. To have an innocent person, some one not in the secret, to play a small part in the comedy of his life, was a desideratum with the artist. His mother had always been this person, this unconscious performer, instinctively falling into the action of the play, and shedding real tears, and smiling actual smiles,—the most useful assistant to a great schemer.

But during the whole of the visit nothing was said as to Paul's conduct towards his unhappy cousin; nothing was said either to praise or to exculpate; and when Mrs. Marchmont and her daughter drove away, in one of the new equipages which Paul had selected for his mother, they left only a vague impression in Belinda's breast. She didn't quite know what to think. These people were so frank and candid, they had spoken of Paul with such real affection, that it was almost impossible to doubt them. Paul Marchmont might be a bad man, but his mother and sister loved him, and surely they were ignorant of his wickedness.

Mrs. Lawford troubled herself very little about this unexpected morning call. She was an excellent, warm-hearted, domestic creature, and thought a great deal more about the grand question as to whether she should have new damask curtains for the drawing-room, or send the old ones to be dyed; or whether she should withdraw her custom from the Kemberling grocer, whose "best black" at four-and-sixpence was really now so very inferior; or whether Belinda's summer silk dress could be cut down into a frock for Isabella to wear in the winter evenings,—than about the rights or wrongs of that story of the horsewhipping which had been administered to Mr. Marchmont.

"I'm sure those Marchmont-Towers people seem very nice, my dear," the lady said to Belinda; "and I really wish your papa would go and dine there. You know I like him to dine out a good deal in the winter, Linda; not that I want to save the housekeeping money,—only it is so difficult to vary the side-dishes for a man who has been accustomed to mess-dinners, and a French cook."

But Belinda stuck fast to her colours. She was a soldier's daughter, as her father said, and she was almost as good as a son. The Major meant this latter remark for very high praise; for the great grief of his life had been the want of a boy's brave face at his fireside. She was as good as a son; that is to say, she was braver and more outspoken than most women; although she was feminine and gentle withal, and by no means strong-minded. She would have fainted, perhaps, at the first sight of blood upon a battle-field; but she would have bled to death with the calm heroism of a martyr, rather than have been false to a noble cause.

"I think papa is quite right not to go to Marchmont Towers, mamma," she said; the artful minx omitted to state that it was by reason of her entreaties her father had stayed away. "I think he is quite right. Mrs. Marchmont and Mrs. Weston may be very nice, and of course it isn't likely *they* would be cruel to poor young Mrs. Arundel; but I *know* that Mr. Marchmont must have been unkind to that poor girl, or Mr. Arundel would never have done what he did."

It is in the nature of good and brave men to lay down their masculine rights when they leave their hats in the hall, and to submit themselves meekly to feminine government. It is only the whippersnapper, the sneak, the coward out of doors who is a tyrant at home. See how meekly the Conqueror of Italy went home to his charming Creole wife! See how pleasantly the Liberator of Italy lolls in the carriage of his golden-haired Empress, when the young trees in that fair wood beyond the triumphal arch are green in the bright spring weather, and all the hired vehicles in Paris are making towards the cascade! Major Lawford's wife was too gentle, and too busy with her store-room and her domestic cares, to tyrannise over her lord and master; but the Major was duly henpecked by his blue-eyed daughters, and went here and there as they dictated.

So he stayed away from Marchmont Towers to please Belinda; and only said, "Haw," "Yes," "'Pon my honour, now!" "Bless my soul!" when his friends told him of the magnificence of Paul's dinners.

But although the Major and his eldest daughter did not encounter Mr. Marchmont in his own house, they met him sometimes on the neutral ground of other people's dining-rooms, and upon one especial evening at a pleasant little dinner-party given by the rector of the parish in which the Grange was situated.

Paul made himself particularly agreeable upon this occasion; but in the brief interval before dinner he was absorbed in a conversation with Mr. Davenant, the rector, upon the subject of ecclesiastical architecture,—he knew everything, and could talk about everything, this dear Paul,—and made no attempt to approach Miss Lawford. He only looked at her now and then, with a furtive, oblique glance out of his almond-shaped, pale-grey eyes; a glance that was wisely hidden by the light auburn lashes, for it had an unpleasant resemblance to the leer of an evil-natured sprite. Mr. Marchmont contented himself with keeping this furtive watch upon Belinda, while she talked gaily with the Rector's two daughters in a pleasant corner near the piano. And as the artist took Mrs. Davenant down to the dining-room, and sat next her at dinner, he had no opportunity of fraternising with Belinda during that meal; for the young lady was divided from him by the whole length of the table and, moreover, very much occupied by the exclusive attentions of two callow-looking officers from the nearest garrison-town, who were afflicted with extreme youth, and were painfully conscious of their degraded state, but tried notwithstanding to carry it off with a high hand, and affected the opinions of used-up fifty.

Mr. Marchmont had none of his womankind with him at this dinner; for his mother and invalid sister had neither of them felt strong enough to come, and Mr. and Mrs. Weston had not been invited. The artist's special object in coming to this dinner was the conquest of Miss Belinda Lawford: she sided with Edward Arundel against him: she must be made to believe Edward wrong, and himself right; or she might go about spreading her opinions, and doing him mischief. Beyond that, he had another idea about Belinda; and he looked to this dinner as likely to afford him an opportunity of laying the foundation of a very diplomatic scheme, in which Miss Lawford should unconsciously become his tool. He was vexed at being placed apart from her at the dinner-table, but he concealed his vexation; and he was aggravated by the Rector's old-fashioned hospitality, which detained the gentlemen over their wine for some time after the ladies left the dining-room. But the opportunity that he wanted came nevertheless, and in a manner that he had not anticipated.

The two callow defenders of their country had sneaked out of the dining-room, and rejoined the ladies in the cosy countrified drawing-rooms. They had stolen away, these two young men; for they were oppressed by the weight of a fearful secret. *They couldn't drink claret!* No; they had tried to like it; they had smacked their lips and winked their eyes—both at once, for even winking with *one* eye is an accomplishment scarcely compatible with extreme youth—over vintages that had seemed to them like a happy admixture of red ink and green-gooseberry juice. They had perjured their boyish souls with hideous falsehoods as to their appreciation of pale tawny port, light dry wines, '42-ports, '45-ports, Kopke Roriz, Thompson and Croft's, and Sandemann's; when, in the secret recesses of their minds, they affected sweet and "slab" compounds, sold by publicans, and facetiously called "Our prime old port, at four-and-sixpence." They were very young, these beardless soldiers. They liked strawberry ices, and were on the verge of insolvency from a predilection for clammy bath-buns, jam-tarts, and cherry-brandy. They liked gorgeous waistcoats; and varnished boots in a state of virgin brilliancy; and little bouquets in their button-holes; and a deluge of *millefleurs* upon their flimsy handkerchiefs. They were very young. The men they met at dinner-parties to-day had tipped them at Eton or Woolwich only yesterday, as it seemed, and remembered it and despised them. It was only a few months since they had been snubbed for calling the Douro a mountain in Switzerland, and the Himalayas a cluster of islands in the Pacific, at horrible examinations, in which the cold perspiration had bedewed their pallid young cheeks. They were delighted to get away from those elderly creatures in the Rector's dining-room to the snug little back drawing-room, where Belinda Lawford and the two Misses Davenant were murmuring softly in the firelight, like young turtles in a sheltered dove-cote; while the matrons in the larger apartment sipped their coffee, and conversed in low awful voices about the iniquities of housemaids, and the insubordination of gardeners and grooms.

Belinda and her two companions were very polite to the helpless young wanderers from the dining-room; and they talked pleasantly enough of all manner of things; until somehow or other the conversation came round to the Marchmont-Towers scandal, and Edward's treatment of his lost wife's kinsman.

One of the young men had been present at the hunting-breakfast on that bright October morning, and he was not a little proud of his superior acquaintance with the whole business.

"I was the-aw, Miss Lawford," he said. "I was on the tew-wace after bweakfast,—and a vewy excellent bweakfast it was, I ass-haw you; the still Moselle was weally admiwable, and Marchmont has some Medewa that immeasuwably surpasses anything I can indooce my wine-merchant to send me;—I was on the tew-wace, and I saw Awundel comin' up the steps, awful pale, and gwasping his whip; and I was a witness of all the west that occurred; and if I had been Marchmont I should have shot Awundel befaw he left the pawk, if I'd had to swing for it, Miss Lawford; for I should have felt, b'Jove, that my own sense of honaw demanded the sacwifice. Howevaw, Marchmont seems a vewy good fella; so I suppose it's all wight as far as he goes; but it was a bwutal business altogethaw, and that fella Awundel must be a scoundwel."

Belinda could not bear this. She had borne a great deal already. She had been obliged to sit by very often, and hear Edward Arundel's conduct discussed by

Thomas, Richard, and Henry, or anybody else who chose to talk about it; and she had been patient, and had held her peace, with her heart bumping indignantly in her breast, and passionate crimson blushes burning her cheeks. But she could *not* submit to hear a beardless, pale-faced, and rather weak-eyed young ensign—who had never done any greater service for his Queen and country than to cry "SHUDDRUPH!" to a detachment of raw recruits in a barrack-yard, in the early bleakness of a winter's morning—take upon himself to blame Edward Arundel, the brave soldier, the noble Indian hero, the devoted lover and husband, the valiant avenger of his dead wife's wrongs.

"I don't think you know anything of the real story, Mr. Palliser," Belinda said boldly to the half-fledged ensign. "If you did, I'm sure you would admire Mr. Arundel's conduct instead of blaming it. Mr. Marchmont fully deserved the disgrace which Edward—which Mr. Arundel inflicted upon him."

The words were still upon her lips, when Paul Marchmont himself came softly through the flickering firelight to the low chair upon which Belinda sat. He came behind her, and laying his hand lightly upon the scroll-work at the back of her chair, bent over her, and said, in a low confidential voice,—

"You are a noble girl, Miss Lawford. I am sorry that you should think ill of me: but I like you for having spoken so frankly. You are a most noble girl. You are worthy to be your father's daughter."

This was said with a tone of suppressed emotion; but it was quite a random shot. Paul didn't know anything about the Major, except that he had a comfortable income, drove a neat dog-cart, and was often seen riding on the flat Lincolnshire roads with his eldest daughter. For all Paul knew to the contrary, Major Lawford might have been the veriest bully and coward who ever made those about him miserable; but Mr. Marchmont's tone as good as expressed that he was intimately acquainted with the old soldier's career, and had long admired and loved him. It was one of Paul's happy inspirations, this allusion to Belinda's father; one of those bright touches of colour laid on with a skilful recklessness, and giving sudden brightness to the whole picture; a little spot of vermilion dabbed upon the canvas with the point of the palette-knife, and lighting up all the landscape with sunshine.

"You know my father?" said Belinda, surprised.

"Who does not know him?" cried the artist. "Do you think, Miss Lawford, that it is necessary to sit at a man's dinner-table before you know what he is? I know your father to be a good man and a brave soldier, as well as I know that the Duke of Wellington is a great general, though I never dined at Apsley House. I respect your father, Miss Lawford; and I have been very much distressed by his evident avoidance of me and mine."

This was coming to the point at once. Mr. Marchmont's manner was candour itself. Belinda looked at him with widely-opened, wondering eyes. She was looking for the evidence of his wickedness in his face. I think she half-expected that Mr. Marchmont would have corked eyebrows, and a slouched hat, like a stage ruffian. She was so innocent, this simple young Belinda, that she imagined wicked people must necessarily look wicked.

Paul Marchmont saw the wavering of her mind in that half-puzzled expression, and he went on boldly.

"I like your father, Miss Lawford," he said; "I like him, and I respect him; and I want to know him. Other people may misunderstand me, if they please. I can't help their opinions. The truth is generally strongest in the end; and I can afford to wait. But I can_not_ afford to forfeit the friendship of a man I esteem; I cannot afford to be misunderstood by your father, Miss Lawford; and I have been very much pained—yes, very much pained—by the manner in which the Major has repelled my little attempts at friendliness."

Belinda's heart smote her. She knew that it was her influence that had kept her father away from Marchmont Towers. This young lady was very conscientious. She was a Christian, too; and a certain sentence touching wrongful judgments rose up against her while Mr. Marchmont was speaking. If she had wronged this man; if Edward Arundel has been misled by his passionate grief for Mary; if she had been deluded by Edward's error,—how very badly Mr. Marchmont had been treated between them! She didn't say anything, but sat looking thoughtfully at the fire; and Paul saw that she was more and more perplexed. This was just what the artist wanted. To talk his antagonist into a state of intellectual fog was almost always his manner of commencing an argument.

Belinda was silent, and Paul seated himself in a chair close to hers. The callow ensigns had gone into the lamp-lit front drawing-room, and were busy turning over the leaves—and never turning them over at the right moment—of a thundering duet which the Misses Davenant were performing for the edification of their papa's visitors. Miss Lawford and Mr. Marchmont were alone, therefore, in that cosy inner chamber, and a very pretty picture they made: the rosy-cheeked girl and the pale, sentimental-looking artist sitting side by side in the glow of the low fire, with a background of crimson curtains and gleaming picture-frames; winter flowers piled in grim Indian jars; the fitful light flickering now and then upon one sharp angle of the high carved mantelpiece, with all its litter of antique china; and the rest of the room in sombre shadow. Paul had the field all to himself, and felt that victory would be easy. He began to talk about Edward Arundel.

If he had said one word against the young soldier, I think this impetuous girl, who had not yet learned to count the cost of what she did, would have been passionately eloquent in defence of her friend's brother—for no other reason than that he was the brother of her friend, of course; what other reason should she have for defending Mr. Arundel?

But Paul Marchmont did not give her any occasion for indignation. On the contrary, he spoke in praise of the hot-headed young soldier who had assaulted him, making all manner of excuses for the young man's violence, and using that tone of calm superiority with which a man of the world might naturally talk about a foolish boy.

"He has been very unreasonable, Miss Lawford," Paul said by-and-by; "he has been very unreasonable, and has most grossly insulted me. But, in spite of all, I believe him to be a very noble young fellow, and I cannot find it in my heart to be really angry with him. What his particular grievance against me may be, I really do not know."

The furtive glance from the long narrow grey eyes kept close watch upon Belinda's face as Paul said this. Mr. Marchmont wanted to ascertain exactly how much Belinda knew of that grievance of Edward's; but he could see only perplexity in her face. She knew nothing definite, therefore; she had only heard Edward talk vaguely of his wrongs. Paul Marchmont was convinced of this; and he went on boldly now, for he felt that the ground was all clear before him.

"This foolish young soldier chooses to be angry with me because of a calamity which I was as powerless to avert, as to prevent that accident upon the South-Western Railway by which Mr. Arundel so nearly lost his life. I cannot tell you how sincerely I regret the misconception that has arisen in his mind. Because I have profited by the death of John Marchmont's daughter, this impetuous young husband imagines—what? I cannot answer that question; nor can he himself, it seems, since he has made no definite statement of his wrongs to any living being."

The artist looked more sharply than ever at Belinda's listening face. There was no change in its expression; the same wondering look, the same perplexity,—that was all.

"When I say that I regret the young man's folly, Miss Lawford," Paul continued, "believe me, it is chiefly on his account rather than my own. Any insult which he can inflict upon me can only rebound upon himself, since everybody in Lincolnshire knows that I am in the right, and he in the wrong."

Mr. Marchmont was going on very smoothly; but at this point Miss Lawford, who had by no means deserted her colours, interrupted his easy progress.

"It remains to be proved who is right and who wrong, Mr. Marchmont," she said. "Mr. Arundel is the brother of my friend. I cannot easily believe him to have done wrong."

Paul looked at her with a smile—a smile that brought hot blushes to her face; but she returned his look without flinching. The brave girl looked full into the narrow grey eyes sheltered under pale auburn lashes, and her steadfast gaze did not waver.

"Ah, Miss Lawford," said the artist, still smiling, "when a young man is handsome, chivalrous, and generous-hearted, it is very difficult to convince a woman that he can do wrong. Edward Arundel has done wrong. His ultra-quixotism has made him blind to the folly of his own acts. I can afford to forgive him. But I repeat that I regret his infatuation about this poor lost girl far more upon his account than on my own; for I know—at least I venture to think—that a way lies open to him of a happier and a better life than he could ever have known with my poor childish cousin Mary Marchmont. I have reason to know that he has formed another attachment, and that it is only a chivalrous delusion about that poor girl—whom he was never really in love with, and whom he only married because of some romantic notion inspired by my cousin John—that withholds him from that other and brighter prospect."

He was silent for a few moments, and then he said hastily,—

"Pardon me, Miss Lawford; I have been betrayed into saying much that I had better have left unsaid, more especially to you. I——"

He hesitated a little, as if embarrassed; and then rose and looked into the next room, where the duet had been followed by a solo.

One of the Rector's daughters came towards the inner drawing-room, followed by a callow ensign.

"We want Belinda to sing," exclaimed Miss Davenant. "We want you to sing, you tiresome Belinda, instead of hiding yourself in that dark room all the evening."

Belinda came out of the darkness, with her cheeks flushed and her eyelids drooping. Her heart was beating so fast as to make it quite impossible to speak just yet, or to sing either. But she sat down before the piano, and, with hands that trembled in spite of herself, began to play one of her pet sonatas.

Unhappily, Beethoven requires precision of touch in the pianist who is bold enough to seek to interpret him; and upon this occasion I am compelled to admit that Miss Lawford's fingering was eccentric, not to say ridiculous,—in common parlance, she made a mess of it; and just as she was going to break down, friendly Clara Davenant cried out,—

"That won't do, Belinda! We want you to sing, not to play. You are trying to cheat us. We would rather have one of Moore's melodies than all Beethoven's sonatas."

So Miss Lawford, still blushing, with her eyelids still drooping, played Sir John Stevenson's simple symphony, and in a fresh swelling voice, that filled the room with melody, began:

"Oh, the days are gone when beauty bright
My heart's chain wove;
When my dream of life, from morn till night,
Was love, still love!"

And Paul Marchmont, sitting at the other end of the room turning over Miss Davenant's scrap-book, looked up through his auburn lashes, and smiled at the beaming face of the singer. He felt that he had improved the occasion.

"I am not afraid of Miss Lawford now," he thought to himself.

This candid, fervent girl was only another piece in the schemer's game of chess; and he saw a way of making her useful in the attainment of that great end which, in the strange simplicity of cunning, he believed to be the one purpose of *every* man's life,—Self-Aggrandisement.

It never for a moment entered into his mind that Edward Arundel was any more *real* than he was himself. There can be no perfect comprehension where there is no sympathy. Paul believed that Edward had tried to become master of Mary Marchmont's heritage; and had failed; and was angry because of his failure. He believed this passionate young man to be a schemer like himself; only a little more impetuous and blundering in his manner of going to work.

CHAPTER V.

THE RETURN OF THE WANDERER.

The March winds were blowing amongst the oaks in Dangerfield Park, when Edward Arundel went back to the house which had never been his home since his boyhood. He went back because he had grown weary of lonely wanderings in that strange Breton country. He had grown weary of himself and of his own thoughts. He was worn out by the eager desire that devoured him by day and by night,—the passionate yearning to be far away beyond that low Eastern horizon line; away amid the carnage and riot of an Indian battle-field.

So he went back at last to his mother, who had written to him again and again, imploring him to return to her, and to rest, and to be happy in the familiar household where he was beloved. He left his luggage at the little inn where the coach that had brought him from Exeter stopped, and then he walked quietly homewards in the gloaming. The early spring evening was bleak and chill. The blacksmith's fire roared at him as he went by the smithy. All the lights in the queer latticed windows twinkled and blinked at him, as if in friendly welcome to the wanderer. He remembered them all: the quaint, misshapen, lopsided roofs; the tumble-down chimneys; the low doorways, that had sunk down below the level of the village street, until all the front parlours became cellars, and strange pedestrians butted their heads against the flower-pots in the bedroom windows; the withered iron frame and pitiful oil-lamp hung out at the corner of the street, and making a faint spot of feeble light upon the rugged pavement; mysterious little shops in diamond-paned parlour windows, where Dutch dolls and stationery, stale gingerbread and pickled cabbage, were mixed up with wooden pegtops, squares of yellow soap, rickety paper kites, green apples, and string; they were all familiar to him.

It had been a fine thing once to come into this village with Letitia, and buy stale gingerbread and rickety kites of a snuffy old pensioner of his mother's. The kites had always stuck in the upper branches of the oaks, and the gingerbread had invariably choked him; but with the memory of the kites and gingerbread came back all the freshness of his youth, and he looked with a pensive tenderness at the homely little shops, the merchandise flickering in the red firelight, that filled each quaint interior with a genial glow of warmth and colour.

He passed unquestioned by a wicket at the side of the great gates. The firelight was rosy in the windows of the lodge, and he heard a woman's voice singing a monotonous song to a sleepy child. Everywhere in this pleasant England there seemed to be the glow of cottage-fires, and friendliness, and love, and home. The young man sighed as he remembered that great stone mansion far away in dismal Lincolnshire, and thought how happy he might have been in this bleak spring twilight, if he could have sat by Mary Marchmont's side in the western drawing-room, watching the firelight and the shadows trembling on her fair young face.

It never had been; and it never was to be. The happiness of a home; the sweet sense of ownership; the delight of dispensing pleasure to others; all the simple domestic joys which make life beautiful,—had never been known to John Marchmont's daughter, since that early time in which she shared her father's lodging in Oakley Street, and went out in the cold December morning to buy rolls for Edward Arundel's breakfast. From the bay-window of his mother's favourite sitting-room the same red light that he had seen in every lattice in the village streamed out upon the growing darkness of the lawn. There was a half-glass door leading into a little lobby near this sitting-room. Edward Arundel opened it and went in, very quietly. He expected to find his mother and his sister in the room with the bay-window.

The door of this familiar apartment was ajar; he pushed it open, and went in. It was a very pretty room, and all the womanly litter of open books and music, needlework and drawing materials, made it homelike. The firelight flickered upon everything—on the pictures and picture-frames, the black oak paneling, the open piano, a cluster of snowdrops in a tall glass on the table, the scattered worsteds by the embroidery-frame, the sleepy dogs upon the hearth-rug. A young lady stood in the bay-window with her back to the fire. Edward Arundel crept softly up to her, and put his arm round her waist.

"Letty!"

It was not Letitia, but a young lady with very blue eyes, who blushed scarlet, and turned upon the young man rather fiercely; and then recognising him, dropped into the nearest chair and began to tremble and grow pale.

"I am sorry I startled you, Miss Lawford," Edward said, gently; "I really thought you were my sister. I did not even know that you were here."

"No, of course not. I—you didn't startle me much, Mr. Arundel; only you were not expected home. I thought you were far away in Brittany. I had no idea that there was any chance of your returning. I thought you meant to be away all the summer—Mrs. Arundel told me so."

Belinda Lawford said all this in that fresh girlish voice which was familiar to Mr. Arundel; but she was still very pale, and she still trembled a little, and there was something almost apologetic in the way in which she assured Edward that she had believed he would be abroad throughout the summer. It seemed almost as if she had said: "I did not come here because I thought I should see you. I had no thought or hope of meeting you."

But Edward Arundel was not a coxcomb, and he was very slow to understand any such signs as these. He saw that he had startled the young lady, and that she had turned pale and trembled as she recognised him; and he looked at her with a half-wondering, half-pensive expression in his face.

She blushed as he looked at her. She went to the table and began to gather together the silks and worsteds, as if the arrangement of her workbasket were a matter of vital importance, to be achieved at any sacrifice of politeness. Then, suddenly remembering that she ought to say something to Mr. Arundel, she gave evidence of the originality of her intellect by the following remark:

"How surprised Mrs. Arundel and Letitia will be to see you!"

Even as she said this her eyes were still bent upon the skeins of worsted in her hand.

"Yes; I think they will be surprised. I did not mean to come home until the autumn. But I got so tired of wandering about a strange country alone. Where are they—my mother and Letitia?"

"They have gone down the village, to the school. They will be back to tea. Your brother is away; and we dine at three o'clock, and drink tea at eight. It is so much pleasanter than dining late."

This was quite an effort of genius; and Miss Lawford went on sorting the skeins of worsted in the firelight. Edward Arundel had been standing all this time with his hat in his hand, almost as if he had been a visitor making a late morning call upon Belinda; but he put his hat down now, and seated himself near the table by which the young lady stood, busy with the arrangement of her workbasket.

Her heart was beating very fast, and she was straining her arithmetical powers to the uttermost, in the endeavour to make a very abstruse calculation as to the time in which Mrs. Arundel and Letitia could walk to the village schoolhouse and back to Dangerfield, and the delay that might arise by reason of sundry interruptions from obsequious gaffers and respectful goodies, eager for a word of friendly salutation from their patroness.

The arrangement of the workbasket could not last for ever. It had become the most pitiful pretence by the time Miss Lawford shut down the wicker lid, and seated herself primly in a low chair by the fireplace. She sat looking down at the fire, and twisting a slender gold chain in and out between her smooth white fingers. She looked very pretty in that fitful firelight, with her waving brown hair pushed off her forehead, and her white eyelids hiding the tender blue eyes. She sat twisting the chain in her fingers, and dared not lift her eyes to Mr. Arundel's face; and if there had been a whole flock of geese in the room, she could not have said "Bo!" to one of them.

And yet she was not a stupid girl. Her father could have indignantly refuted any such slander as that against the azure-eyed Hebe who made his home pleasant to him. To the Major's mind Belinda was all that man could desire in the woman of his choice, whether as daughter or wife. She was the bright genius of the old man's home, and he loved her with that chivalrous devotion which is common to brave soldiers, who are the simplest and gentlest of men when you chain them to their firesides, and keep them away from the din of the camp and the confusion of the transport-ship.

Belinda Lawford was clever; but only just clever enough to be charming. I don't think she could have got through "Paradise Lost," or Gibbon's "Decline and Fall," or a volume by Adam Smith or McCulloch, though you had promised her a diamond necklace when she came conscientiously to "Finis." But she could read Shakespeare for the hour together, and did read him aloud to her father in a fresh, clear voice, that was like music on the water. And she read Macaulay's "History of England," with eyes that kindled with indignation against cowardly, obstinate James, or melted with pity for poor weak foolish Monmouth, as the case might be. She could play Mendelssohn and Beethoven,—plaintive sonatas; tender songs, that had no need of words to expound the mystic meaning of the music. She could sing old ballads and Irish melodies, that thrilled the souls of those who heard her, and made hard men pitiful to brazen Hibernian beggars in the London streets for the memory of that pensive music. She could read the leaders in the "Times," with no false quantities in the Latin quotations, and knew what she was reading about; and had her favourites at St. Stephen's; and adored Lord Palmerston, and was liberal to the core of her tender young heart. She was as brave as a true Englishwoman should be, and would have gone to the wars with her old father, and served him as his page; or would have followed him into captivity, and tended him in prison, if she had lived in the days when there was such work for a high-spirited girl to do.

But she sat opposite Mr. Edward Arundel, and twisted her chain round her fingers, and listened for the footsteps of the returning mistress of the house. She was like a bashful schoolgirl who has danced with an officer at her first ball. And yet amidst her shy confusion, her fears that she should seem agitated and embarrassed, her struggles to appear at her ease, there was a sort of pleasure in being seated there by the low fire with Edward Arundel opposite to her. There was a strange pleasure, an almost painful pleasure, mingled with her feelings in those quiet moments. She was acutely conscious of every sound that broke the stillness—the sighing of the wind in the wide chimney; the falling of the cinders on the hearth; the occasional snort of one of the sleeping dogs; and the beating of her own restless heart. And though she dared not lift her eyelids to the young soldier's face, that handsome, earnest countenance, with the chestnut hair lit up with gleams of gold, the firm lips shaded by a brown moustache, the pensive smile, the broad white forehead, the dark-blue handkerchief tied loosely under a white collar, the careless grey travelling-dress, even the attitude of the hand and arm, the bent head drooping a little over the fire,—were as present to her inner sight as if her eyes had kept watch all this time, and had never wavered in their steady gaze.

There is a second-sight that is not recognised by grave professors of magic—a second-sight which common people call Love.

But by-and-by Edward began to talk, and then Miss Lawford found courage, and took heart to question him about his wanderings in Brittany. She had only been a few weeks in Devonshire, she said. Her thoughts went back to the dreary autumn in Lincolnshire as she spoke; and she remembered the dull October day upon which her father had come into the girl's morning-room at the Grange with Edward's farewell letter in his hand. She remembered this, and all the talk that there had been about the horsewhipping of Mr. Paul Marchmont upon his own threshold. She remembered all the warm discussions, the speculations, the ignorant conjectures, the praise, the blame; and how it had been her business to sit by and listen and hold her peace, except upon that one never-to-be-forgotten night at the Rectory, when Paul Marchmont had hinted at something whose perfect meaning she had never dared to imagine, but which had, somehow or other, mingled vaguely with all her day-dreams ever since.

Was there any truth in that which Paul Marchmont had said to her? Was it true that Edward Arundel had never really loved his young bride?

Letitia had said as much, not once, but twenty times.

"It's quite ridiculous to suppose that he could have ever been in love with the poor, dear, sickly thing," Miss Arundel had exclaimed; "it was only the absurd romance of the business that captivated him; for Edward is really ridiculously romantic, and her father having been a supernumer—(it's no use, I don't think anybody ever did know how many syllables there are in that word)—and having lived in Oakley Street, and having written a pitiful letter to Edward, about this motherless daughter and all that sort of thing, just like one of those tiresome old novels with a baby left at a cottage-door, and all the *s*'s looking like *f*'s, and the last word of one page repeated at the top of the next page, and printed upon thick yellow-looking ribbed paper, you know. *That* was why my brother married Miss Marchmont, you may depend upon it, Linda; and all I hope is, that he'll be sensible enough to marry again soon, and to have a Christianlike wedding, with carriages, and a breakfast, and two clergymen; and *I* should wear white glacé silk, with tulle puffings, and a tulle bonnet (I suppose I must wear a bonnet, being only a bridesmaid?), all showered over with clematis, as if I'd stood under a clematis-bush when the wind was blowing, you know, Linda."

With such discourse as this Miss Arundel had frequently entertained her friend; and she had indulged in numerous inuendoes of an embarrassing nature as to the propriety of old friends and schoolfellows being united by the endearing tie of sister-in-lawhood, and other observations to the like effect.

Belinda knew that if Edward ever came to love her,—whenever she did venture to speculate upon such a chance, she never dared to come at all near it, but thought of it as a thing that might come to pass in half a century or so— if he should choose her for his second wife, she knew that she would be gladly and tenderly welcomed at Dangerfield. Mrs. Arundel had hinted as much as this. Belinda knew how anxiously that loving mother hoped that her son might, by-and-by, form new ties, and cease to lead a purposeless life, wasting his brightest years in lamentations for his lost bride: she knew all this; and sitting opposite to the young man in the firelight, there was a dull pain at her heart; for there was something in the soldier's sombre face that told her he had not yet ceased to lament that irrevocable past.

But Mrs. Arundel and Letitia came in presently, and gave utterance to loud rejoicings; and preparations were made for the physical comfort of the wanderer,—bells were rung, lighted wax-candles and a glittering tea-service were brought in, a cloth was laid, and cold meats and other comestibles spread forth, with that profusion which has made the west country as proverbial as the north for its hospitality. I think Miss Lawford would have sat opposite the traveller for a week without asking any such commonplace question as to whether Mr. Arundel required refreshment. She had read in her Hort's "Pantheon" that the gods sometimes ate and drank like ordinary mortals; yet it had never entered into her mind that Edward could be hungry. But she now had the satisfaction of seeing Mr. Arundel eat a very good dinner; while she herself poured out the tea, to oblige Letitia, who was in the middle of the third volume of a new novel, and went on reading it as coolly as if there had been no such person as that handsome young soldier in the world.

"The books must go back to the club to-morrow morning, you know, mamma dear, or I wouldn't read at tea-time," the young lady remarked apologetically.

"I want to know whether *he'll* marry Theodora or that nasty Miss St. Ledger. Linda thinks he'll marry Miss St. Ledger, and be miserable, and Theodora will die. I believe Linda likes love-stories to end unhappily. I don't. I hope if he *does* marry Miss St. Ledger—and he'll be a wicked wretch if he does, after the *things* he has said to Theodora—I hope, if he does, she'll die—catch cold at a *déjeuner* at Twickenham, or something of that kind, you know; and then he'll marry Theodora afterwards, and all will end happily. Do you know, Linda, I always fancy that you're like Theodora, and that Edward's like *him*."

After which speech Miss Arundel went back to her book, and Edward helped himself to a slice of tongue rather awkwardly, and Belinda Lawford, who had her hand upon the urn, suffered the teapot to overflow amongst the cups and saucers.

CHAPTER VI.

For some time after his return Edward Arundel was very restless and gloomy: roaming about the country by himself, under the influence of a pretended passion for pedestrianism; reading hard for the first time in his life, shutting himself in his dead father's library, and sitting hour after hour in a great easy-chair, reading the histories of all the wars that have ever ravaged this earth—from the days in which the elephants of a Carthaginian ruler trampled upon the soldiery of Rome, to the era of that Corsican barrister's wonderful son, who came out of his simple island home to conquer the civilised half of a world.

Edward Arundel showed himself a very indifferent brother; for, do what she would, Letitia could not induce him to join in any of her pursuits. She caused a butt to be set up upon the lawn; but all she could say about Belinda's "best gold" could not bring the young man out upon the grass to watch the two girls shooting. He looked at them by stealth sometimes through the window of the library, and sighed as he thought of the blight upon his manhood, and of all the things that might have been.

Might not these things even yet come to pass? Had he not done his duty to the dead; and was he not free now to begin a fresh life? His mother was perpetually hinting at some bright prospect that lay smiling before him, if he chose to take the blossom-bestrewn path that led to that fair country. His sister told him still more plainly of a prize that was within his reach, if he were but brave enough to stretch out his hand and claim the precious treasure for his own. But when he thought of all this,—when he pondered whether it would not be wise to drop the dense curtain of forgetfulness over that sad picture of the past,—whether it would not be well to let the dead bury their dead, and to accept that other blessing which the same Providence that had blighted his first hope seemed to offer to him now,—the shadowy phantom of John Marchmont arose out of the mystic realms of the dead, and a ghostly voice cried to him, "I charged you with my daughter's safe keeping; I trusted you with her innocent love; I gave you the custody of her helplessness. What have you done to show yourself worthy of my faith in you?"

These thoughts tormented the young widower perpetually, and deprived him of all pleasure in the congenial society of his sister and Belinda Lawford; or infused so sharp a flavour of remorse into his cup of enjoyment, that pleasure was akin to pain.

So I don't know how it was that, in the dusky twilight of a bright day in early May, nearly two months after his return to Dangerfield, Edward Arundel, coming by chance upon Miss Lawford as she sat alone in the deep bay-window where he had found her on his first coming, confessed to her the terrible struggle of feeling that made the great trouble of his life, and asked her if she was willing to accept a love which, in its warmest fervour, was not quite unclouded by the shadows of the sorrowful past.

"I love you dearly, Linda," he said; "I love, I esteem, I admire you; and I know that it is in your power to give me the happiest future that ever a man imagined in his youngest, brightest dreams. But if you do accept my love, dear, you must take my memory with it. I cannot forget, Linda. I have tried to forget. I have prayed that God, in His mercy, might give me forgetfulness of that irrevocable past. But the prayer has never been granted; the boon has never been bestowed. I think that love for the living and remorse for the dead must for ever reign side by side in my heart. It is no falsehood to you that makes me remember her; it is no forgetfulness of her that makes me love you. I offer my brighter and happier self to you, Belinda; I consecrate my sorrow and my tears to her. I love you with all my heart, Belinda; but even for the sake of your love I will not pretend that I can forget her. If John Marchmont's daughter had died with her head upon my breast, and a prayer on her lips, I might have regretted her as other men regret their wives; and I might have learned by-and-by to look back upon my grief with only a tender and natural regret, that would have left my future life unclouded. But it can never be so. The poison of remorse is blended with that sorrowful memory. If I had done otherwise,—if I had been wiser and more thoughtful,—my darling need never have suffered; my darling need never have sinned. It is the thought that her death may have been a sinful one, that is most cruel to me, Belinda. I have seen her pray, with her pale earnest face uplifted, and the light of faith shining in her gentle eyes; I have seen the inspiration of God upon her face; and I cannot bear to think that, in the darkness that came down upon her young life, that holy light was quenched; I cannot bear to think that Heaven was ever deaf to the pitiful cry of my innocent lamb."

And here Mr. Arundel paused, and sat silently, looking out at the long shadows of the trees upon the darkening lawn; and I fear that, for the time being, he forgot that he had just made Miss Lawford an offer of his hand, and so much of his heart as a widower may be supposed to have at his disposal.

Ah me! we can only live and die *once*. There are some things, and those the most beautiful of all things, that can never be renewed: the bloom on a butterfly's wing; the morning dew upon a newly-blown rose; our first view of the ocean; our first pantomime, when all the fairies were fairies for ever, and when the imprudent consumption of the contents of a pewter quart-measure in sight of the stage-box could not disenchant us with that elfin creature, Harlequin the graceful, faithful betrothed of Columbine the fair. The firstlings of life are most precious. When the black wing of the angel of death swept over agonised Egypt, and the children were smitten, offended Heaven, eager for a sacrifice, took the firstborn. The young mothers would have other children, perhaps; but between those others and the mother's love there would be the pale shadow of that lost darling whose tiny hands *first* drew undreamed-of melodies from the sleeping chords, *first* evoked the slumbering spirit of maternal love. Amongst the later lines—the most passionate, the most sorrowful—that George Gordon Noel Byron wrote, are some brief verses that breathed a lament for the lost freshness, the never-to-be-recovered youth.

"Oh, could I feel as I have felt; or be what I have been;
 Or weep as I could once have wept!"

cried the poet, when he complained of that "mortal coldness of the soul," which is "like death itself." It is a pity certainly that so great a man should die in the prime of life; but if Byron had survived to old age after writing these lines, he would have been a living anticlimax. When a man writes that sort of poetry he pledges himself to die young.

Edward Arundel had grown to love Belinda Lawford unconsciously, and in spite of himself; but the first love of his heart, the first fruit of his youth, had perished. He could not feel quite the same devotion, the same boyish chivalry, that he had felt for the innocent bride who had wandered beside him in the sheltered meadows near Winchester. He might begin a *new* life, but he could not live the *old* life over again. He must wear his rue with a difference this time. But he loved Belinda very dearly, nevertheless; and he told her so, and by-and-by won from her a tearful avowal of affection.

Alas! she had no power to question the manner of his wooing. He loved her—he had said as much; and all the good she had desired in this universe became hers from the moment of Edward Arundel's utterance of those words. He loved her; that was enough. That he should cherish a remorseful sorrow for that lost wife, made him only the truer, nobler, and dearer in Belinda's sight. She was not vain, or exacting, or selfish. It was not in her nature to begrudge poor dead Mary the tender thoughts of her husband. She was generous, impulsive, believing; and she had no more inclination to doubt Edward's love for her, after he had once avowed such a sentiment, than to disbelieve in the light of heaven when she saw the sun shining. Unquestioning, and unutterably happy, she received her lover's betrothal kiss, and went with him to his mother, blushing and trembling, to receive that lady's blessing.

"Ah, if you knew how I have prayed for this, Linda!" Mrs. Arundel exclaimed, as she folded the girl's slight figure in her arms.

"And I shall wear white glacé with pinked flounces, instead of tulle puffings, you sly Linda," cried Letitia.

"And I'll give Ted the home-farm, and the white house to live in, if he likes to try his hand at the new system of farming," said Reginald Arundel, who had come home from the Continent, and had amused himself for the last week by strolling about his estate and staring at his timber, and almost wishing that there was a necessity for cutting down all the oaks in the avenue, so that he might have something to occupy him until the 12th of August.

Never was promised bride more welcome to a household than bright Belinda Lawford; and as for the young lady herself, I must confess that she was almost childishly happy, and that it was all that she could do to prevent her light step from falling into a dance as she floated hither and thither through the house at Dangerfield,—a fresh young Hebe in crisp muslin robes; a gentle goddess, with smiles upon her face and happiness in her heart.

"I loved you from the first, Edward," she whispered one day to her lover. "I knew that you were good, and brave, and noble; and I loved you because of that."

And a little for the golden glimmer in his clustering curls; and a little for his handsome profile, his flashing eyes, and that distinguished air peculiar to the defenders of their country; more especially peculiar, perhaps, to those who ride on horseback when they sally forth to defend her. Once a soldier for ever a soldier, I think. You may rob the noble warrior of his uniform, if you will; but the *je ne sais quoi*, the nameless air of the "long-sword, saddle, bridle," will hang round him still.

Mrs. Arundel and Letitia took matters quite out of the hands of the two lovers. The elderly lady fixed the wedding-day, by agreement with Major Lawford, and sketched out the route for the wedding-tour. The younger lady chose the fabrics for the dresses of the bride and her attendants; and all was done before Edward and Belinda well knew what their friends were about. I think that Mrs. Arundel feared her son might change his mind if matters were not brought swiftly to a climax, and that she hurried on the irrevocable day in order that he might have no breathing time until the vows had been spoken and Belinda Lawford was his wedded wife. It had been arranged that Edward should escort Belinda back to Lincolnshire, and that his mother and Letitia, who was to be chief bridesmaid, should go with them. The marriage was to be solemnised at Hillingsworth church, which was within a mile and a half of the Grange.

The 1st of July was the day appointed by agreement between Major and Mrs. Lawford and Mrs. Arundel; and on the 18th of June Edward was to accompany his mother, Letitia, and Belinda to London. They were to break the journey by stopping in town for a few days, in order to make a great many purchases necessary for Miss Lawford's wedding paraphernalia, for which the Major had sent a bouncing cheque to his favourite daughter.

And all this time the only person at all unsettled, the only person whose mind was ill at ease, was Edward Arundel, the young widower who was about to take to himself a second wife. His mother, who watched him with a maternal comprehension of every change in his face, saw this, and trembled for her son's happiness.

"And yet he cannot be otherwise than happy with Belinda Lawford," Mrs. Arundel thought to herself.

But upon the eve of that journey to London Edward sat alone with his mother in the drawing-room at Dangerfield, after the two younger ladies had retired for the night. They slept in adjoining apartments, these two young ladies; and I regret to say that a great deal of their conversation was about Valenciennes lace, and flounces cut upon the cross, moire antique, mull muslin, glacé silk, and the last "sweet thing" in bonnets. It was only when loquacious Letitia was shut out that Miss Lawford knelt alone in the still moonlight, and prayed that she might be a good wife to the man who had chosen her. I don't think she ever prayed that she might be faithful and true and pure; for it never entered into her mind that any creature bearing the sacred name of wife could be otherwise. She only prayed for the mysterious power to preserve her husband's affection, and make his life happy.

Mrs. Arundel, sitting *tête-à-tête* with her younger son in the lamp-lit drawing-room, was startled by hearing the young man breathe a deep sigh. She looked up from her work to see a sadder expression in his face than perhaps ever clouded the countenance of an expectant bridegroom.

"Edward!" she exclaimed.

"What, mother?"

"How heavily you sighed just now!"

"Did I?" said Mr. Arundel, abstractedly. Then, after a brief pause, he said, in a different tone, "It is no use trying to hide these things from you, mother. The truth is, I am not happy."

"Not happy, Edward!" cried Mrs. Arundel; "but surely you——?"

"I know what you are going to say, mother. Yes, mother, I love this dear girl

Linda with all my heart; I love her most sincerely; and I could look forward to a life of unalloyed happiness with her, if—if there was not some inexplicable dread, some vague and most miserable feeling always coming between me and my hopes. I have tried to look forward to the future, mother; I have tried to think of what my life may be with Belinda; but I cannot, I cannot. I cannot look forward; all is dark to me. I try to build up a bright palace, and an unknown hand shatters it. I try to turn away from the memory of my old sorrows; but the same hand plucks me back, and chains me to the past. If I could retract what I have done; if I could, with any show of honour, draw back, even now, and not go upon this journey to Lincolnshire; if I *could* break my faith to this poor girl who loves me, and whom I love, as God knows, with all truth and earnestness, I would do so—I would do so."

"Edward!"

"Yes, mother; I would do it. It is not in me to forget. My dead wife haunts me by night and day. I hear her voice crying to me, 'False, false, false; cruel and false; heartless and forgetful!' There is never a night that I do not dream of that dark sluggish river down in Lincolnshire. There is never a dream that I have—however purposeless, however inconsistent in all its other details—in which I do not see *her* dead face looking up at me through the murky waters. Even when I am talking to Linda, when words of love for her are on my lips, my mind wanders away, back—always back—to the sunset by the boat-house, when my little wife gave me her hand; to the trout-stream in the meadow, where we sat side by side and talked about the future."

For a few minutes Mrs. Arundel was quite silent. She abandoned herself for that brief interval to complete despair. It was all over. The bridegroom would cry off; insulted Major Lawford would come post-haste to Dangerfield, to annihilate this dismal widower, who did not know his own mind. All the shimmering fabrics—the gauzes, and laces, and silks, and velvets—that were in course of preparation in the upper chambers would become so much useless finery, to be hidden in out-of-the-way cupboards, and devoured by misanthropical moths,—insect iconoclasts, who take a delight in destroying the decorations of the human temple.

Poor Mrs. Arundel took a mental photograph of all the complicated horrors of the situation. An offended father; a gentle, loving girl crushed like some broken lily; gossip, slander; misery of all kinds. And then the lady plucked up courage and gave her recreant son a sound lecture, to the effect that this conduct was atrociously wicked; and that if this trusting young bride, this fair young second wife, were to be taken away from him as the first had been, such a calamity would only be a fitting judgment upon him for his folly.

But Edward told his mother, very quietly, that he had no intention of being false to his newly-plighted troth.

"I love Belinda," he said; "and I will be true to her, mother. But I cannot forget the past; it hangs about me like a bad dream."

CHAPTER VII.

The young widower made no further lamentation, but did his duty to his betrothed bride with a cheerful visage. Ah! what a pleasant journey it was to Belinda, that progress through London on the way to Lincolnshire! It was like that triumphant journey of last March, when the Royal bridegroom led his Northern bride through a surging sea of eager, smiling faces, to the musical jangling of a thousand bells. If there were neither populace nor joy-bells on this occasion, I scarcely think Miss Lawford knew that those elements of a triumphal progress were missing. To her ears all the universe was musical with the sound of mystic joy-bells; all the earth was glad with the brightness of happy faces. The railway-carriage,—the commonplace vehicle,—frouzy with the odour of wool and morocco, was a fairy chariot, more wonderful than Queen Mab's; the white chalk-cutting in the hill was a shining cleft in a mountain of silver; the wandering streams were melted diamonds; the stations were enchanted castles. The pale sherry, carried in a pocket-flask, and sipped out of a little silver tumbler—there is apt to be a warm flatness about sherry taken out of pocket-flasks that is scarcely agreeable to the connoisseur—was like nectar newly brewed for the gods; even the anchovies in the sandwiches were like the enchanted fish in the Arabian story. A magical philter had been infused into the atmosphere: the flavour of first love was in every sight and sound.

Was ever bridegroom more indulgent, more devoted, than Edward Arundel? He sat at the counters of silk-mercers for the hour together, while Mrs. Arundel and the two girls deliberated over crisp fabrics unfolded for their inspection. He was always ready to be consulted, and gave his opinion upon the conflicting merits of peach-colour and pink, apple-green and maize, with unwearying attention. But sometimes, even while Belinda was smiling at him, with the rippling silken stuff held up in her white hands, and making a lustrous cascade upon the counter, the mystic hand plucked him back, and his mind wandered away to that childish bride who had chosen no splendid garments for her wedding, but had gone with him to the altar as trustfully as a baby goes in its mother's arms to the cradle. If he had been left alone with Belinda, with tender, sympathetic Belinda,—who loved him well enough to understand him, and was always ready to take her cue from his face, and to be joyous or thoughtful according to his mood,—it might have been better for him. But his mother and Letitia reigned paramount during this ante-nuptial week, and Mr. Arundel was scarcely suffered to take breath. He was hustled hither and thither in the hot summer noontide. He was taken to choose a dressing-case for his bride; and he was made to look at glittering objects until his eyes ached, and he could see nothing but a bewildering dazzle of ormolu and silver-gilt. He was taken to a great emporium in Bond Street to select perfumery, and made to sniff at divers essences until his nostrils were unnaturally distended, and his olfactory nerves afflicted with temporary paralysis. There was jewellery of his mother and of Belinda's mother to be re-set; and the hymeneal victim was compelled to sit for an hour or so, blinking at fiery-crested serpents that were destined to coil up his wife's arms, and emerald padlocks that were to lie upon her breast. And then, when his soul was weary of glaring splendours and glittering confusions, they took him round the Park, in a whirlpool of diaphanous bonnets, and smiling faces, and brazen harness, and emblazoned hammer-cloths, on the margin of a river whose waters were like molten gold under the blazing sun. And then they gave him a seat in an opera-box, and the crash of a monster orchestra, blended with the hum of a thousand voices, to soothe his nerves withal.

But the more wearied this young man became with glitter, and dazzle, and sunshine, and silk-mercer's ware, the more surely his mind wandered back to the still meadows, and the limpid trout-stream, the sheltering hills, the solemn shadows of the cathedral, the distant voices of the rooks high up in the waving elms.

The bustle of preparation was over at last, and the bridal party went down to Lincolnshire. Pleasant chambers had been prepared at the Grange for Mr. Arundel and his mother and sister; and the bridegroom was received with enthusiasm by Belinda's blue-eyed younger sisters, who were enchanted to find that there was going to be a wedding and that they were to have new frocks.

So Edward would have been a churl indeed had he seemed otherwise than happy, had he been anything but devoted to the bright girl who loved him.

Tidings of the coming wedding flew like wildfire through Lincolnshire. Edward Arundel's romantic story had elevated him into a hero; all manner of reports had been circulated about his devotion to his lost young wife. He had sworn never to mingle in society again, people said. He had sworn never to have a new suit of clothes, or to have his hair cut, or to shave, or to eat a hot dinner. And Lincolnshire by no means approved of the defection implied by his approaching union with Belinda. He was only a commonplace widower, after all, it seemed; ready to be consoled as soon as the ceremonious interval of decent grief was over. People had expected something better of him. They had expected to see him in a year or two with long grey hair, dressed in shabby raiment, and, with his beard upon his breast, prowling about the village of Kemberling, baited by little children. Lincolnshire was very much disappointed by the turn that affairs had taken. Shakesperian aphorisms were current among the gossips at comfortable tea-tables; and people talked about funeral baked meats, and the propriety of building churches if you have any ambitious desire that your memory should outlast your life; and indulged in other bitter observations, familiar to all admirers of the great dramatist.

But there were some people in Lincolnshire to whom the news of Edward Arundel's intended marriage was more welcome than the early May-flowers to rustic children eager for a festival. Paul Marchmont heard the report, and rubbed his hands stealthily, and smiled to himself as he sat reading in the sunny western drawing-room. The good seed that he had sown that night at the Rectory had borne this welcome fruit. Edward Arundel with a young wife would be very much less formidable than Edward Arundel single and discontented, prowling about the neighbourhood of Marchmont Towers, and perpetually threatening vengeance upon Mary's cousin.

It was busy little Lavinia Weston who first brought her brother the tidings. He took both her hands in his, and kissed them in his enthusiasm.

"My best of sisters," he said, "you shall have a pair of diamond earrings for this."

"For only bringing you the news, Paul?"

"For only bringing me the news. When a messenger carries the tidings of a great victory to his king, the king makes him a knight upon the spot. This marriage is a victory to me, Lavinia. From to-day I shall breathe freely."

"But they are not married yet. Something may happen, perhaps, to prevent ____"

"What should happen?" asked Paul, rather sharply. "By-the-bye, it will be as well to keep this from Mrs. John," he added, thoughtfully; "though really now I fancy it matters very little what she hears."

He tapped his forehead lightly with his two slim fingers, and there was a horrible significance in the action.

"She is not likely to hear anything," Mrs. Weston said; "she sees no one but Barbara Simmons."

"Then I should be glad if you would give Simmons a hint to hold her tongue. This news about the wedding would disturb her mistress."

"Yes, I'll tell her so. Barbara is a very excellent person. I can always manage Barbara. But oh, Paul, I don't know what I'm to do with that poor weak-witted husband of mine."

"How do you mean?"

"Oh, Paul, I have had such a scene with him to-day—such a scene! You remember the way he went on that day down in the boat-house when Edward Arundel came in upon us unexpectedly? Well, he's been going on as badly as that to-day, Paul,—or worse, I really think."

Mr. Marchmont frowned, and flung aside his newspaper, with a gesture expressive of considerable vexation.

"Now really, Lavinia, this is too bad," he said; "if your husband is a fool, I am not going to be bored about his folly. You have managed him for fifteen years: surely you can go on managing him now without annoying *me* about him? If Mr. George Weston doesn't know when he's well off, he's an ungrateful cur, and you may tell him so, with my compliments."

He picked up his newspaper again, and began to read. But Lavinia Weston, looking anxiously at her brother's face, saw that his pale auburn brows were contracted in a thoughtful frown, and that, if he read at all, the words upon which his eyes rested could convey very little meaning to his brain.

She was right; for presently he spoke to her, still looking at the page before him, and with an attempt at carelessness.

"Do you think that fellow would go to Australia, Lavinia?"

"Alone?" asked his sister.

"Yes, alone of course," said Mr. Marchmont, putting down his paper, and looking at Mrs. Weston rather dubiously. "I don't want you to go to the Antipodes; but if—if the fellow refused to go without you, I'd make it well worth your while to go out there, Lavinia. You shouldn't have any reason to regret obliging me, my dear girl."

The dear girl looked rather sharply at her affectionate brother.

"It's like your selfishness, Paul, to propose such a thing," she said, "after all I've done——!"

"I have not been illiberal to you, Lavinia."

"No; you've been generous enough to me, I know, in the matter of gifts; but you're rich, Paul, and you can afford to give. I don't like the idea that you're so willing to pack me out of the way now that I can be no longer useful to you."

Mr. Marchmont shrugged his shoulders.

"For Heaven's sake, Lavinia, don't be sentimental. If there's one thing I despise more than another, it is this kind of mawkish sentimentality. You've been a very good sister to me; and I've been a very decent brother to you. If you have served me, I have made it answer your purpose to do so. I don't want you to go away. You may bring all your goods and chattels to this house to-morrow, if you like, and live at free quarters here for the rest of your existence. But if George Weston is a pig-headed brute, who can't understand upon which side his bread is buttered, he must be got out of the way somehow. I don't care what it costs me; but he must be got out of the way. I'm not going to live the life of a modern Damocles, with a blundering sword always dangling over my head, in the person of Mr. George Weston. And if the man objects to leave the country without you, why, I think your going with him would be only a sisterly act towards me. I hate selfishness, Lavinia, almost as much as I detest sentimentality."

Mrs. Weston was silent for some minutes, absorbed in reflection. Paul got up, kicked aside a footstool, and walked up and down the room with his hands in his pockets.

"Perhaps I might get George to leave England, if I promised to join him as soon as he was comfortably settled in the colonies," Mrs. Weston said, at last.

"Yes," cried Paul; "nothing could be more easy. I'll act very liberally towards him, Lavinia; I'll treat him well; but he shall not stay in England. No, Lavinia; after what you have told me to-day, I feel that he must be got out of the country."

Mr. Marchmont went to the door and looked out, to see if by chance any one had been listening to him. The coast was quite clear. The stone-paved hall looked as desolate as some undiscovered chamber in an Egyptian temple. The artist went back to Lavinia, and seated himself by her side. For some time the brother and sister talked together earnestly.

They settled everything for poor henpecked George Weston. He was to sail for Sydney immediately. Nothing could be more easy than for Lavinia to declare that her brother had accidentally heard of some grand opening for a medical practitioner in the metropolis of the Antipodes. The surgeon was to have a very handsome sum given him, and Lavinia would *of course* join him as soon as he was settled. Paul Marchmont even looked through the "Shipping Gazette" in search of an Australian vessel which should speedily convey his brother-in-law to a distant shore.

Lavinia Weston went home armed with all necessary credentials. She was to promise almost anything to her husband, provided that he gave his consent to an early departure.

CHAPTER VIII.

Upon the 31st of June, the eve of Edward Arundel's wedding-day, Olivia Marchmont sat in her own room,—the room that she had chiefly occupied ever since her husband's death,—the study looking out into the quadrangle. She sat alone in that dismal chamber, dimly lighted by a pair of wax-candles, in tall tarnished silver candlesticks. There could be no greater contrast than that between this desolate woman and the master of the house. All about him was bright and fresh, and glittering and splendid; around her there was only ruin and decay, thickening dust and gathering cobwebs,—outward evidences of an inner wreck. John Marchmont's widow was of no importance in that household. The servants did not care to trouble themselves about her whims or wishes, nor to put her rooms in order. They no longer curtseyed to her when they met her, wandering—with a purposeless step and listless feet that dragged along the ground—up and down the corridor, or out in the dreary quadrangle. What was to be gained by any show of respect to her, whose brain was too weak to hold the memory of their conduct for five minutes together?

Barbara Simmons only was faithful to her mistress with an unvarying fidelity. She made no boast of her devotion; she expected neither fee nor reward for her self-abnegation. That rigid religion of discipline which had not been strong enough to preserve Olivia's stormy soul from danger and ruin was at least all-sufficient for this lower type of woman. Barbara Simmons had been taught to do her duty, and she did it without question or complaint. As she went through rain, snow, hail, or sunshine twice every Sunday to Kemberling church,—as she sat upon a cushionless seat in an uncomfortable angle of the servants' pew, with the sharp edges of the woodwork cutting her thin shoulders, to listen patiently to dull rambling sermons upon the hardest texts of St. Paul,—so she attended upon her mistress, submitting to every caprice, putting up with every hardship; because it was her duty so to do. The only relief she allowed herself was an hour's gossip now and then in the housekeeper's room; but she never alluded to her mistress's infirmities, nor would it have been safe for any other servant to have spoken lightly of Mrs. John Marchmont in stern Barbara's presence.

Upon this summer evening, when happy people were still lingering amongst the wild flowers in shady lanes, or in the dusky pathways by the quiet river, Olivia sat alone, staring at the candles.

Was there anything in her mind; or was she only a human automaton, slowly decaying into dust? There was no speculation in those large lustreless eyes, fixed upon the dim light of the candles. But, for all that, the mind was not a blank. The pictures of the past, for ever changing like the scenes in some magic panorama, revolved before her. She had no memory of that which had happened a quarter of an hour ago; but she could remember every word that Edward Arundel had said to her in the Rectory-garden at Swampington,— every intonation of the voice in which those words had been spoken.

There was a tea-service on the table: an attenuated little silver teapot; a lopsided cream-jug, with thin worn edges and one dumpy little foot missing; and an antique dragon china cup and saucer with the gilding washed off. That meal, which is generally called social, has but a dismal aspect when it is only prepared for one. The solitary teacup, half filled with cold, stagnant tea, with a leaf or two floating upon the top, like weeds on the surface of a tideless pond; the teaspoon, thrown askew across a little pool of spilt milk in the tea-tray,—looked as dreary as the ruins of a deserted city.

In the western drawing-room Paul was strolling backwards and forwards, talking to his mother and sisters, and admiring his pictures. He had spent a great deal of money upon art since taking possession of the Towers, and the western drawing-room was quite a different place to what it had been in John Marchmont's lifetime.

Etty's divinities smiled through hazy draperies, more transparent than the summer vapours that float before the moon. Pearly-complexioned nymphs, with faces archly peeping round the corner of soft rosy shoulders, frolicked amidst the silver spray of classic fountains. Turner's Grecian temples glimmered through sultry summer mists; while glimpses of ocean sparkled here and there, and were as beautiful as if the artist's brush had been dipped in melted opals. Stanfield's breezy beaches made cool spots of freshness on the wall, and sturdy sailor-boys, with their hands up to their mouths and their loose hair blowing in the wind, shouted to their comrades upon the decks of brown-sailed fishing-smacks. Panting deer upon dizzy crags, amid the misty Highlands, testified to the hand of Landseer. Low down, in the corners of the room, there lurked quaint cottage-scenes by Faed and Nichol. Ward's patched and powdered beaux and beauties,—a Rochester, in a light perriwig; a Nell Gwynne, showing her white teeth across a basket of oranges; a group of *Incroyables*, with bunches of ribbons hanging from their low topboots, and two sets of dangling seals at their waists—made a blaze of colour upon the walls: and amongst all these glories of to-day there were prim Madonnas and stiff-necked angels by Raphael and Tintoretto; a brown-faced grinning boy by Murillo (no collection ever was complete without that inevitable brown-faced boy); an obese Venus, by the great Peter Paul; and a pale Charles the First, with martyrdom foreshadowed in his pensive face, by Vandyke.

Paul Marchmont contemplated his treasures complacently, as he strolled about the room, with his coffee-cup in his hand; while his mother watched him admiringly from her comfortable cushioned nest at one end of a luxurious sofa.

"Well, mother," Mr. Marchmont said presently, "let people say what they may of me, they can never say that I have used my money badly. When I am dead and gone, these pictures will remain to speak for me; posterity will say, 'At any rate the fellow was a man of taste.' Now what, in Heaven's name, could that miserable little Mary have done with eleven thousand a year, if—if she had lived to enjoy it?"

* * * * *

The minute-hand of the little clock in Mrs. John Marchmont's study was creeping slowly towards the quarter before eleven, when Olivia was aroused suddenly from that long reverie, in which the images of the past had shone upon her across the dull stagnation of the present like the domes and minarets in a Phantasm City gleaming athwart the barren desert-sands.

She was aroused by a cautious tap upon the outside of her window. She got up, opened the window, and looked out. The night was dark and starless, and there was a faint whisper of wind among the trees.

"Don't be frightened," whispered a timid voice; "it's only me, George Weston. I want to talk to you, Mrs. John. I've got something particular to tell you—awful particular; but *they* mustn't hear it; *they* mustn't know I'm here. I came round this way on purpose. You can let me in at the little door in the lobby, can't you, Mrs. John? I tell you, I must tell you what I've got to tell you," cried Mr. Weston, indifferent to tautology in his excitement. "Do let me in, there's a dear good soul. The little door in the lobby, you know; it's locked, you know, but I dessay the key's there."

"The door in the lobby?" repeated Olivia, in a dreamy voice.

"Yes, *you* know. Do let me in now, that's a good creature. It's awful particular, I tell you. It's about Edward Arundel."

Edward Arundel! The sound of that name seemed to act upon the woman's shattered nerves like a stroke of electricity. The drooping head reared itself erect. The eyes, so lustreless before, flashed fire from their sombre depths. Comprehension, animation, energy returned; as suddenly as if the wand of an enchanter had summoned the dead back to life.

61

"Edward Arundel!" she cried, in a clear voice, which was utterly unlike the dull deadness of her usual tones.

"Hush," whispered Mr. Weston; "don't speak loud, for goodness gracious sake. I dessay there's all manner of spies about. Let me in, and I'll tell you everything."

"Yes, yes; I'll let you in. The door by the lobby—I understand; come, come."

Olivia disappeared from the window. The lobby of which the surgeon had spoken was close to her own apartment. She found the key in the lock of the door. The place was dark; she opened the door almost noiselessly, and Mr. Weston crept in on tiptoe. He followed Olivia into the study, closed the door behind him, and drew a long breath.

"I've got in," he said; "and now I am in, wild horses shouldn't hold me from speaking my mind, much less Paul Marchmont."

He turned the key in the door as he spoke, and even as he did so glanced rather suspiciously towards the window. To his mind the very atmosphere of that house was pervaded by the presence of his brother-in-law.

"O Mrs. John!" exclaimed the surgeon, in piteous accents, "the way that I've been trampled upon. *You've* been trampled upon, Mrs. John, but you don't seem to mind it; and perhaps it's better to bring oneself to that, if one can; but I can't. I've tried to bring myself to it; I've even taken to drinking, Mrs. John, much as it goes against me; and I've tried to drown my feelings as a man in rum-and-water. But the more spirits I consume, Mrs. John, the more of a man I feel."

Mr. Weston struck the top of his hat with his clenched fist, and stared fiercely at Olivia, breathing very hard, and breathing rum-and-water with a faint odour of lemon-peel.

"Edward Arundel!—what about Edward Arundel?" said Olivia, in a low eager voice.

"I'm coming to that, Mrs. John, in due c'course," returned Mr. Weston, with an air of dignity that was superior even to hiccough. "What I say, Mrs. John," he added, in a confidential and argumentative tone, "is this: *I won't be trampled upon!*" Here his voice sank to an awful whisper. "Of course it's pleasant enough to have one's rent provided for, and not to be kept awake by poor's-rates, Mrs. John; but, good gracious me! I'd rather have the Queen's taxes and the poor-rates following me up day and night, and a man in possession to provide for at every meal—and you don't know how contemptuous a man in possession can look at you if you offer him salt butter, or your table in a general way don't meet his views—than the conscience I've had since Paul Marchmont came into Lincolnshire. I feel, Mrs. John, as if I'd committed oceans of murders. It's a miracle to me that my hair hasn't turned white before this; and it would have done it, Mrs. J., if it wasn't of that stubborn nature which is too wiry to give expression to a man's sufferings. O Mrs. John, when I think how my pangs of conscience have been made game of,—when I remember the insulting names I have been called, because my heart didn't happen to be made of adamant,—my blood boils; it boils, Mrs. John, to that degree, that I feel the time has come for action. I have been put upon until the spirit of manliness within me blazes up like a fiery furnace. I have been trodden upon, Mrs. John; but I'm not the worm they took me for. To-day they've put the finisher upon it." The surgeon paused to take breath. His mild and rather sheep-like countenance was flushed; his fluffy eyebrows twitched convulsively in his endeavours to give expression to the violence of his feelings. "To-day they've put the finisher upon it," he repeated. "I'm to go to Australia, am I? Ha! ha! we'll see about that. There's a nice opening in the medical line, is there? and dear Paul will provide the funds to start me! Ha! ha! two can play at that game. It's all brotherly kindness, of course, and friendly interest in my welfare—that's what it's *called*, Mrs. J. Shall I tell you what it *is*? I'm to be got rid of, at any price, for fear my conscience should get the better of me, and I should speak. I've been made a tool of, and I've been trampled upon; but they've been *obliged* to trust me. I've got a conscience, and I don't suit their views. If I hadn't got a conscience, I might stop here and have my rent and taxes provided for, and riot in rum-and-water to the end of my days. But I've a conscience that all the pineapple rum in Jamaica wouldn't drown, and they're frightened of me."

Olivia listened to all this with an impatient frown upon her face. I doubt if she knew the meaning of Mr. Weston's complaints. She had been listening only for the one name that had power to transform her from a breathing automaton into a living, thinking, reasoning woman. She grasped the surgeon's wrist fiercely.

"You told me you came here to speak about Edward Arundel," she said. "Have you been only trying to make a fool of me."

"No, Mrs. John; I have come to speak about him, and I come to you, because I think you're not so bad as Paul Marchmont. I think that you've been a tool, like myself; and they've led you on, step by step, from bad to worse, pretty much as they have led me. You're Edward Arundel's blood-relation, and it's your business to look to any wrong that's done him, more than it is mine. But if you don't speak, Mrs. John, I will. Edward Arundel is going to be married."

"Going to be married!" The words burst from Olivia's lips in a kind of shriek, and she stood glaring hideously at the surgeon, with her lips apart and her eyes dilated. Mr. Weston was fascinated by the horror of that gaze, and stared at her in silence for some moments. "You are a madman!" she exclaimed, after a pause; "you are a madman! Why do you come here with your idiotic fancies? Surely my life is miserable enough without this!"

"I ain't mad, Mrs. John, any more than"—Mr. Weston was going to say, "than you are;" but it struck him that, under existing circumstances, the comparison might be ill-advised—"I ain't any madder than other people," he said, presently. "Edward Arundel is going to be married. I have seen the young lady in Kemberling with her pa; and she's a very sweet young woman to look at; and her name is Belinda Lawford; and the wedding is to be at eleven o'clock to-morrow morning at Hillingsworth church."

Olivia slowly lifted her hands to her head, and swept the loose hair away from her brow. All the mists that had obscured her brain melted slowly away, and showed her the past as it had really been in all its naked horror. Yes; step by step the cruel hand had urged her on from bad to worse; from bad to worse; until it had driven her *here*.

It was for *this* that she had sold her soul to the powers of hell. It was for *this* that she had helped to torture that innocent girl whom a dying father had given into her pitiless hand. For this! for this! To find at last that all her iniquity had been wasted, and that Edward Arundel had chosen another bride —fairer, perhaps, than the first. The mad, unholy jealousy of her nature awoke from the obscurity of mental decay, a fierce ungovernable spirit. But another spirit arose in the next moment. CONSCIENCE, which so long had slumbered, awoke and cried to her, in an awful voice, "Sinner, whose sin has been wasted, repent! restore! It is not yet too late."

The stern precepts of her religion came back to her. She had rebelled against those rigid laws, she had cast off those iron fetters, only to fall into a worse bondage; only to submit to a stronger tyranny. She had been a servant of the God of Sacrifice, and had rebelled when an offering was demanded of her. She had cast off the yoke of her Master, and had yielded herself up the slave of sin. And now, when she discovered whither her chains had dragged her, she was seized with a sudden panic, and wanted to go back to her old master.

She stood for some minutes with her open palms pressed upon her forehead, and her chest heaving as if a stormy sea had raged in her bosom.

"This marriage must not take place," she cried, at last.

"Of course it mustn't," answered Mr. Weston; "didn't I say so just now? And if you don't speak to Paul and prevent it, I will. I'd rather you spoke to him, though," added the surgeon thoughtfully, "because, you see, it would come better from you, wouldn't it now?"

Olivia Marchmont did not answer. Her hands had dropped from her head, and she was standing looking at the floor.

"There shall be no marriage," she muttered, with a wild laugh. "There's another heart to be broken—that's all. Stand aside, man," she cried; "stand aside, and let me go to *him*; let me go to him."

She pushed the terrified surgeon out of her pathway, and locked the door, hurried along the passage and across the hall. She opened the door of the western drawing-room, and went in.

Mr. Weston stood in the corridor looking after her. He waited for a few minutes, listening for any sound that might come from the western drawing-room. But the wide stone hall was between him and that apartment; and however loudly the voices might have been uplifted, no breath of them could have reached the surgeon's ear. He waited for about five minutes, and then crept into the lobby and let himself out into the quadrangle.

"At any rate, nobody can say that I'm a coward," he thought complacently, as he went under a stone archway that led into the park. "But what a whirlwind that woman is! O my gracious, what a perfect whirlwind she is!"

CHAPTER IX.

Paul Marchmont was still strolling hither and thither about the room, admiring his pictures, and smiling to himself at the recollection of the easy manner in which he had obtained George Weston's consent to the Australian arrangement. For in his sober moments the surgeon was ready to submit to anything his wife and brother-in-law imposed upon him; it was only under the influence of pineapple rum that his manhood asserted itself. Paul was still contemplating his pictures when Olivia burst into the room; but Mrs. Marchmont and her invalid daughter had retired for the night, and the artist was alone,—alone with his own thoughts, which were rather of a triumphal and agreeable character just now; for Edward's marriage and Mr. Weston's departure were equally pleasant to him.

He was startled a little by Olivia's abrupt entrance, for it was not her habit to intrude upon him or any member of that household; on the contrary, she had shown an obstinate determination to shut herself up in her own room, and to avoid every living creature except her servant Barbara Simmons.

Paul turned and confronted her very deliberately, and with the smile that was almost habitual to him upon his thin pale lips. Her sudden appearance had blanched his face a little; but beyond this he betrayed no sign of agitation.

"My dear Mrs. Marchmont, you quite startle me. It is so very unusual to see you here, and at this hour especially."

It did not seem as if she had heard his voice. She went sternly up to him, with her thin listless arms hanging at her side, and her haggard eyes fixed upon his face.

"Is this true?" she asked.

He started a little, in spite of himself; for he understood in a moment what she meant. Some one, it scarcely mattered who, had told her of the coming marriage.

"Is what true, my dear Mrs. John?" he said carelessly.

"Is this true that George Weston tells me?" she cried, laying her thin hand upon his shoulder. Her wasted fingers closed involuntarily upon the collar of his coat, her lips contracted into a ghastly smile, and a sudden fire kindled in her eyes. A strange sensation awoke in the tips of those tightening fingers, and thrilled through every vein of the woman's body,—such a horrible thrill as vibrates along the nerves of a monomaniac, when the sight of a dreadful terror in his victim's face first arouses the murderous impulse in his breast.

Paul's face whitened as he felt the thin finger-points tightening upon his neck. He was afraid of Olivia.

"My dear Mrs. John, what is it you want of me?" he said hastily. "Pray do not be violent."

"I am not violent."

She dropped her hand from his breast. It was true, she was not violent. Her voice was low; her hand fell loosely by her side. But Paul was frightened of her, nevertheless; for he saw that if she was not violent, she was something worse—she was dangerous.

"Did George Weston tell me the truth just now?" she said.

Paul bit his nether-lip savagely. George Weston had tricked him, then, after all, and had communicated with this woman. But what of that? She would scarcely be likely to trouble herself about this business of Edward Arundel's marriage. She must be past any such folly as that. She would not dare to interfere in the matter. She could not.

"Is it true?" she said; "*is* it? Is it true that Edward Arundel is going to be married to-morrow?"

She waited, looking with fixed, widely-opened eyes at Paul's face.

"My dear Mrs. John, you take me so completely by surprise, that I——"

"That you have not got a lying answer ready for me," said Olivia, interrupting him. "You need not trouble yourself to invent one. I see that George Weston told me the truth. There was reality in his words. There is nothing but falsehood in yours."

Paul stood looking at her, but not listening to her. Let her abuse and upbraid him to her heart's content; it gave him leisure to reflect, and plan his course of action; and perhaps these bitter words might exhaust the fire within her, and leave her malleable to his skilful hands once more. He had time to think this, and to settle his own line of conduct while Olivia was speaking to him. It was useless to deny the marriage. She had heard of it from George Weston, and she might hear of it from any one else whom she chose to interrogate. It was useless to try to stifle this fact.

"Yes, Mrs. John," he said, "it is quite true. Your cousin, Mr. Arundel, is going to marry Belinda Lawford; a very lucky thing for us, believe me, as it will put an end to all questioning and watching and suspicion, and place us beyond all danger."

67

Olivia looked at him, with her bosom heaving, her breath growing shorter and louder with every word he spoke.

"You mean to let this be, then?" she said, when he had finished speaking.

"To let what be?"

"This marriage. You will let it take place?"

"Most certainly. Why should I prevent it?"

"Why should you prevent it?" she cried fiercely; and then, in an altered voice, in tones of anguish that were like a wail of despair, she exclaimed, "O my God! my God! what a dupe I have been; what a miserable tool in this man's hands! O my offended God! why didst Thou so abandon me, when I turned away from Thee, and made Edward Arundel the idol of my wicked heart?"

Paul sank into the nearest chair, with a faint sigh of relief.

"She will wear herself out," he thought, "and then I shall be able to do what I like with her."

But Olivia turned to him again while he was thinking this.

"Do you imagine that *I* will let this marriage take place?" she asked.

"I do not think that you will be so mad as to prevent it. That little mystery which you and I have arranged between us is not exactly child's play, Mrs. John. We can neither of us afford to betray the other. Let Edward Arundel marry, and work for his wife, and be happy; nothing could be better for us than his marriage. Indeed, we have every reason to be thankful to Providence for the turn that affairs have taken," Mr. Marchmont concluded, piously.

"Indeed!" said Olivia; "and Edward Arundel is to have another bride. He is to be happy with another wife; and I am to hear of their happiness, to see him some day, perhaps, sitting by her side and smiling at her, as I have seen him smile at Mary Marchmont. He is to be happy, and I am to know of his happiness. Another baby-faced girl is to glory in the knowledge of his love; and I am to be quiet—I am to be quiet. Is it for this that I have sold my soul to you, Paul Marchmont? Is it for this I have shared your guilty secrets? Is it for this I have heard *her* feeble wailing sounding in my wretched feverish slumbers, as I have heard it every night, since the day she left this house? Do you remember what you said to me? Do you remember *how* you tempted me? Do you remember how you played upon my misery, and traded on the tortures of my jealous heart? 'He has despised your love,' you said: 'will you consent to see him happy with another woman?' That was your argument, Paul Marchmont. You allied yourself with the devil that held possession of my breast, and together you were too strong for me. I was set apart to be damned,

68

and you were the chosen instrument of my damnation. You bought my soul, Paul Marchmont. You shall not cheat me of the price for which I sold it. You shall hinder this marriage!"

"You are a madwoman, Mrs. John Marchmont, or you would not propose any such thing."

"Go," she said, pointing to the door; "go to Edward Arundel, and do something, no matter what, to prevent this marriage."

"I shall do nothing of the kind."

He had heard that a monomaniac was always to be subdued by indomitable resolution, and he looked at Olivia, thinking to tame her by his unfaltering glance. He might as well have tried to look the raging sea into calmness.

"I am not a fool, Mrs. John Marchmont," he said, "and I shall do nothing of the kind."

He had risen, and stood by the lamp-lit table, trifling rather nervously with its elegant litter of delicately-bound books, jewel-handled paper-knives, newly-cut periodicals, and pretty fantastical toys collected by the women of the household.

The faces of the two were nearly upon a level as they stood opposite to each other, with only the table between them.

"Then *I* will prevent it!" Olivia cried, turning towards the door.

Paul Marchmont saw the resolution stamped upon her face. She would do what she threatened. He ran to the door and had his hand upon the lock before she could reach it.

"No, Mrs. John," he said, standing at the door, with his back turned to Olivia, and his fingers busy with the bolts and key. In spite of himself, this woman had made him a little nervous, and it was as much as he could do to find the handle of the key. "No, no, my dear Mrs. John; you shall not leave this house, nor this room, in your present state of mind. If you choose to be violent and unmanageable, we will give you the full benefit of your violence, and we will give you a better sphere of action. A padded room will be more suitable to your present temper, my dear madam. If you favour us with this sort of conduct, we will find people more fitted to restrain you."

He said all this in a sneering tone that had a trifling tremulousness in it, while he locked the door and assured himself that it was safely secured. Then he turned, prepared to fight out the battle somehow or other.

At the very moment of his turning there was a sudden crash, a shiver of broken glass, and the cold night-wind blew into the room. One of the long

French windows was wide open, and Olivia Marchmont was gone.

He was out upon the terrace in the next moment; but even then he was too late, for he could not see her right or left of him upon the long stone platform. There were three separate flights of steps, three different paths, widely diverging across the broad grassy flat before Marchmont Towers. How could he tell which of these ways Olivia might have chosen? There was the great porch, and there were all manner of stone abutments along the grim façade of the house. She might have concealed herself behind any one of them. The night was hopelessly dark. A pair of ponderous bronze lamps, which Paul had placed before the principal doorway, only made two spots of light in the gloom. He ran along the terrace, looking into every nook and corner which might have served as a hiding-place; but he did not find Olivia.

She had left the house with the avowed intention of doing something to prevent the marriage. What would she do? What course would this desperate woman take in her jealous rage? Would she go straight to Edward Arundel and tell him——?

Yes, this was most likely; for how else could she hope to prevent the marriage?

Paul stood quite still upon the terrace for a few minutes, thinking. There was only one course for him. To try and find Olivia would be next to hopeless. There were half-a-dozen outlets from the park. There were ever so many different pathways through the woody labyrinth at the back of the Towers. This woman might have taken any one of them. To waste the night in searching for her would be worse than useless.

There was only one thing to be done. He must countercheck this desperate creature's movements.

He went back to the drawing-room, shut the window, and then rang the bell.

There were not many of the old servants who had waited upon John Marchmont at the Towers now. The man who answered the bell was a person whom Paul had brought down from London.

"Get the chesnut saddled for me, Peterson," said Mr. Marchmont. "My poor cousin's widow has left the house, and I am going after her. She has given me very great alarm to-night by her conduct. I tell you this in confidence; but you can say as much to Mrs. Simmons, who knows more about her mistress than I do. See that there's no time lost in saddling the chesnut. I want to overtake this unhappy woman, if I can. Go and give the order, and then bring me my hat."

The man went away to obey his master. Paul walked to the chimneypiece and looked at the clock.

"They'll be gone to bed at the Grange," he thought to himself. "Will she go there and knock them up, I wonder? Does she know that Edward's there? I doubt that; and yet Weston may have told her. At any rate, I can be there before her. It would take her a long time to get there on foot. I think I did the right thing in saying what I said to Peterson. I must have the report of her madness spread everywhere. I must face it out. But how—but how? So long as she was quiet, I could manage everything. But with her against me, and George Weston—oh, the cur, the white-hearted villain, after all that I've done for him and Lavinia! But what can a man expect when he's obliged to put his trust in a fool?"

He went to the window, and stood there looking out until he saw the groom coming along the gravel roadway below the terrace, leading a horse by the bridle. Then he put on the hat that the servant had brought him, ran down the steps, and got into the saddle.

"All right, Jeffreys," he said; "tell them not to expect me back till to-morrow morning. Let Mrs. Simmons sit up for her mistress. Mrs. John may return at any hour in the night."

He galloped away along the smooth carriage-drive. At the lodge he stopped to inquire if any one had been through that way. No, the woman said; she had opened the gates for no one. Paul had expected no other answer. There was a footpath that led to a little wicket-gate opening on the high-road; and of course Olivia had chosen that way, which was a good deal shorter than the carriage-drive.

CHAPTER X.

It was past two o'clock in the morning of the day which had been appointed for Edward Arundel's wedding, when Paul Marchmont drew rein before the white gate that divided Major Lawford's garden from the high-road. There was no lodge, no pretence of grandeur here. An old-fashioned garden surrounded an old-fashioned red-brick house. There was an apple-orchard upon one side of the low white gate, and a flower-garden, with a lawn and fish-pond, upon the other. The carriage-drive wound sharply round to a shallow flight of steps, and a broad door with a narrow window upon each side of it.

Paul got off his horse at the gate, and went in, leading the animal by the bridle. He was a Cockney, heart and soul, and had no sense of any enjoyments that were not of a Cockney nature. So the horse he had selected for himself was anything but a fiery creature. He liked plenty of bone and very little blood in the steed he rode, and was contented to go at a comfortable, jog-trot, seven-miles-an-hour pace, along the wretched country roads.

There was a row of old-fashioned wooden posts, with iron chains swinging between them, upon both sides of the doorway. Paul fastened the horse's bridle to one of these, and went up the steps. He rang a bell that went clanging and jangling through the house in the stillness of the summer night. All the way along the road he had looked right and left, expecting to pass Olivia; but he had seen no sign of her. This was nothing, however; for there were byways by which she might come from Marchmont Towers to Lawford Grange.

"I must be before her, at any rate," Paul thought to himself, as he waited patiently for an answer to his summons.

The time seemed very long to him, of course; but at last he saw a light glimmering through the mansion windows, and heard a shuffling foot in the hall. Then the door was opened very cautiously, and a woman's scared face peered out at Mr. Marchmont through the opening.

"What is it?" the woman asked, in a frightened voice.

"It is I, Mr. Marchmont, of Marchmont Towers. Your master knows me. Mr. Arundel is here, is he not?"

"Yes, and Mrs. Arundel too; but they're all abed."

"Never mind that; I must see Major Lawford immediately."

"But they're all abed."

"Never mind that, my good woman; I tell you I must see him."

"But won't to-morrow mornin' do? It's near three o'clock, and to-morrow's our eldest miss's weddin'-day; and they're all abed."

"I *must* see your master. For mercy's sake, my good woman, do what I tell you! Go and call up Major Lawford,—you can do it quietly,—and tell him I must speak to him at once."

The woman, with the chain of the door still between her and Mr. Marchmont, took a timid survey of Paul's face. She had heard of him often enough, but had never seen him before, and she was rather doubtful as to his identity. She knew that thieves and robbers resorted to all sorts of tricks in the course of their evil vocation. Mightn't this application for admittance in the dead of the night be only a part of some burglarious plot against the spoons and forks, and that hereditary silver urn with lions' heads holding rings in their mouths for handles, the fame of which had no doubt circulated throughout all Lincolnshire? Mr. Marchmont had neither a black mask nor a dark-lantern, and to Martha Philpot's mind these were essential attributes of the legitimate burglar; but he might be burglariously disposed, nevertheless, and it would be well to be on the safe side.

"I'll go and tell 'em," the discreet Martha said civilly; "but perhaps you won't mind my leaving the chain oop. It ain't like as if it was winter," she added apologetically.

"You may shut the door, if you like," answered Paul; "only be quick and wake your master. You can tell him that I want to see him upon a matter of life and death."

Martha hurried away, and Paul stood upon the broad stone steps waiting for her return. Every moment was precious to him, for he wanted to be beforehand with Olivia. He had no thought except that she would come straight to the Grange to see Edward Arundel; unless, indeed, she was by any chance ignorant of his whereabouts.

Presently the light appeared again in the narrow windows, and this time a man's foot sounded upon the stone-flagged hall. This time, too, Martha let down the chain, and opened the door wide enough for Mr. Marchmont to enter. She had no fear of burglarious marauders now that the valiant Major was at her elbow.

"Mr. Marchmont," exclaimed the old soldier, opening a door leading into a little study, "you will excuse me if I seem rather bewildered by your visit. When an old fellow like me is called up in the middle of the night, he can't be expected to have his wits about him just at first. (Martha, bring us a light.) Sit down, Mr. Marchmont; there's a chair at your elbow. And now may I ask the reason——?"

"The reason I have disturbed you in this abrupt manner. The occasion that brings me here is a very painful one; but I believe that my coming may save you and yours from much annoyance."

"Save us from annoyance! Really, my dear sir, you——"

"I mystify you for the moment, no doubt," Paul interposed blandly; "but if you will have a little patience with me, Major Lawford, I think I can make everything very clear,—only too painfully clear. You have heard of my relative, Mrs. John Marchmont,—my cousin's widow?"

"I have," answered the Major, gravely.

The dark scandals that had been current about wretched Olivia Marchmont came into his mind with the mention of her name, and the memory of those miserable slanders overshadowed his frank face.

Paul waited while Martha brought in a smoky lamp, with the half-lighted wick sputtering and struggling in its oily socket. Then he went on, in a calm, dispassionate voice, which seemed the voice of a benevolent Christian, sublimely remote from other people's sorrows, but tenderly pitiful of suffering humanity, nevertheless.

"You have heard of my unhappy cousin. You have no doubt heard that she is —mad?"

He dropped his voice into so low a whisper, that he only seemed to shape this last word with his thin flexible lips.

"I have heard some rumour to that effect," the Major answered; "that is to say, I have heard that Mrs. John Marchmont has lately become eccentric in her habits."

"It has been my dismal task to watch the slow decay of a very powerful intellect," continued Paul. "When I first came to Marchmont Towers, about the time of my cousin Mary's unfortunate elopement with Mr. Arundel, that mental decay had already set in. Already the compass of Olivia Marchmont's mind had become reduced to a monotone, and the one dominant thought was doing its ruinous work. It was my fate to find the clue to that sad decay; it was my fate very speedily to discover the nature of that all-absorbing thought which, little by little, had grown into monomania."

Major Lawford stared at his visitor's face. He was a plain-spoken man, and could scarcely see his way clearly through all this obscurity of fine words.

74

"You mean to say you found out what had driven your cousin's widow mad?" he said bluntly.

"You put the question very plainly, Major Lawford. Yes; I discovered the secret of my unhappy relative's morbid state of mind. That secret lies in the fact, that for the last ten years Olivia Marchmont has cherished a hopeless affection for her cousin, Mr. Edward Arundel."

The Major almost bounded off his chair in horrified surprise.

"Good gracious!" he exclaimed; "you surprise me, Mr. Marchmont, and—and —rather unpleasantly."

"I should never have revealed this secret to you or to any other living creature, Major Lawford, had not circumstances compelled me to do so. As far as Mr. Arundel is concerned, I can set your mind quite at ease. He has chosen to insult me very grossly; but let that pass. I must do him the justice to state that I believe him to have been from first to last utterly ignorant of the state of his cousin's mind."

"I hope so, sir; egad, I hope so!" exclaimed the Major, rather fiercely. "If I thought that this young man had trifled with the lady's affection; if I thought ———"

"You need think nothing to the detriment of Mr. Arundel," answered Paul, with placid politeness, "except that he is hot-headed, obstinate, and foolish. He is a young man of excellent principles, and has never fathomed the secret of his cousin's conduct towards him. I am rather a close observer,— something of a student of human nature,—and I have watched this unhappy woman. She loves, and has loved, her cousin Edward Arundel; and hers is one of those concentrative natures in which a great passion is nearly akin to a monomania. It was this hopeless, unreturned affection that embittered her character, and made her a harsh stepmother to my poor cousin Mary. For a long time this wretched woman has been very quiet; but her tranquillity has been only a deceitful calm. To-night the storm broke. Olivia Marchmont heard of the marriage that is to take place to-morrow; and, for the first time, a state of melancholy mania developed into absolute violence. She came to me, and attacked me upon the subject of this intended marriage. She accused me of having plotted to give Edward Arundel another bride; and then, after exhausting herself by a torrent of passionate invective against me, against her cousin Edward, your daughter,—every one concerned in to-morrow's event, —this wretched woman rushed out of the house in a jealous fury, declaring that she would do something—no matter what—to hinder the celebration of Edward Arundel's second marriage."

"Good Heavens!" gasped the Major. "And you mean to say———"

"I mean to say, that there is no knowing what may be attempted by a madwoman, driven mad by a jealousy in itself almost as terrible as madness. Olivia Marchmont has sworn to hinder your daughter's marriage. What has not been done by unhappy creatures in this woman's state of mind? Every day we read of such things in the newspapers—deeds of horror at which the blood grows cold in our veins; and we wonder that Heaven can permit such misery. It is not any frivolous motive that brings me here in the dead of the night, Major Lawford. I come to tell you that a desperate woman has sworn to hinder to-morrow's marriage. Heaven knows what she may do in her jealous frenzy! She *may* attack your daughter."

The father's face grew pale. His Linda, his darling, exposed to the fury of a madwoman! He could conjure up the scene: the fair girl clinging to her lover's breast, and desperate Olivia Marchmont swooping down upon her like an angry tigress.

"For mercy's sake, tell me what I am to do, Mr. Marchmont!" cried the Major. "God bless you, sir, for bringing me this warning! But what am I to do? What do you advise? Shall we postpone the wedding?"

"On no account. All you have to do is to keep this wretched woman at bay. Shut your doors upon her. Do not let her be admitted to this house upon any pretence whatever. Get the wedding over an hour earlier than has been intended, if it is possible for you to do so, and hurry the bride and bridegroom away upon the first stage of their wedding-tour. If you wish to escape all the wretchedness of a public scandal, avoid seeing this woman."

"I will, I will," answered the bewildered Major. "It's a most awful situation. My poor Belinda! Her wedding-day! And a mad woman to attempt—Upon my word, Mr. Marchmont, I don't know how to thank you for the trouble you have taken."

"Don't speak of that. This woman is my cousin's widow: any shame of hers is disgrace to me. Avoid seeing her. If by any chance she does contrive to force herself upon you, turn a deaf ear to all she may say. She horrified me to-night by her mad assertions. Be prepared for anything she may declare. She is possessed by all manner of delusions, remember, and may make the most ridiculous assertions. There is no limit to her hallucinations. She may offer to bring Edward Arundel's dead wife from the grave, perhaps. But you will not, on any account, allow her to obtain access to your daughter."

"No, no—on no account. My poor Belinda! I am very grateful to you, Mr. Marchmont, for this warning. You'll stop here for the rest of the night? Martha's beds are always aired. You'll accept the shelter of our spare room until to-morrow morning?"

"You are very good, Major Lawford; but I must hurry away directly. Remember that I am quite ignorant as to where my unhappy relative may be wandering at this hour of the night. She may have returned to the Towers. Her jealous fury may have exhausted itself; and in that case I have exaggerated the danger. But, at any rate I thought it best to give you this warning."

"Most decidedly, my dear sir; I thank you from the bottom of my heart. But you'll take something—wine, tea, brandy-and-water—eh?"

Paul had put on his hat and made his way into the hall by this time. There was no affectation in his eagerness to be away. He glanced uneasily towards the door every now and then while the Major was offering hospitable hindrance to his departure. He was very pale, with a haggard, ashen pallor that betrayed his anxiety, in spite of his bland calmness of manner.

"You are very kind. No; I will get away at once. I have done my duty here; I must now try and do what I can for this wretched woman. Good night. Remember; shut your doors upon her."

He unfastened the bridle of his horse, mounted, and rode away slowly, so long as there was any chance of the horse's tread being heard at the Grange. But when he was a quarter of a mile away from Major Lawford's house, he urged the horse into a gallop. He had no spurs; but he used his whip with a ruthless hand, and went off at a tearing pace along a narrow lane, where the ruts were deep.

He rode for fifteen miles; and it was grey morning when he drew rein at a dilapidated five-barred gate leading into the great, tenantless yard of an uninhabited farmhouse. The place had been unlet for some years; and the land was in the charge of a hind in Mr. Marchmont's service. The hind lived in a cottage at the other extremity of the farm; and Paul had erected new buildings, with engine-houses and complicated machinery for pumping the water off the low-lying lands. Thus it was that the old farmhouse and the old farmyard were suffered to fall into decay. The empty sties, the ruined barns and outhouses, the rotting straw, and pools of rank corruption, made this tenantless farmyard the very abomination of desolation. Paul Marchmont opened the gate and went in. He picked his way very cautiously through the mud and filth, leading his horse by the bridle till he came to an outhouse, where he secured the animal. Then he crossed the yard, lifted the rusty latch of a narrow wooden door set in a plastered wall, and went into a dismal stone court, where one lonely hen was moulting in miserable solitude.

Long rank grass grew in the interstices of the flags. The lonely hen set up a roopy cackle, and fluttered into a corner at sight of Paul Marchmont. There were some rabbit-hutches, tenantless; a dovecote, empty; a dog-kennel, and a broken chain rusting slowly in a pool of water, but no dog. The courtyard was at the back of the house, looked down upon by a range of latticed windows, some with closed shutters, others with shutters swinging in the wind, as if they had been fain to beat themselves to death in very desolation of spirit.

Mr. Marchmont opened a door and went into the house. There were empty cellars and pantries, dairies and sculleries, right and left of him. The rats and mice scuttled away at sound of the intruder's footfall. The spiders ran upon the damp-stained walls, and the disturbed cobwebs floated slowly down from the cracked ceilings and tickled Mr. Marchmont's face.

Farther on in the interior of the gloomy habitation Paul found a great stone-paved kitchen, at the darkest end of which there was a rusty grate, in which a minimum of flame struggled feebly with a maximum of smoke. An open oven-door revealed a dreary black cavern; and the very manner of the rusty door, and loose, half-broken handle, was an advertisement of incapacity for any homely hospitable use. Pale, sickly fungi had sprung up in clusters at the corners of the damp hearthstone. Spiders and rats, damp and cobwebs, every sign by which Decay writes its name upon the dwelling man has deserted, had set its separate mark upon this ruined place.

Paul Marchmont looked round him with a contemptuous shudder. He called "Mrs. Brown! Mrs. Brown!" two or three times, each time waiting for an answer; but none came, and Mr. Marchmont passed on into another room.

Here at least there was some poor pretence of comfort. The room was in the front of the house, and the low latticed window looked out upon a neglected garden, where some tall foxgloves reared their gaudy heads amongst the weeds. At the end of the garden there was a high brick wall, with pear-trees trained against it, and dragon's-mouth and wallflower waving in the morning-breeze.

There was a bed in this room, empty; an easy-chair near the window; near that a little table, and a *set of Indian chessmen*. Upon the bed there were some garments scattered, as if but lately flung there; and on the floor, near the fireplace, there were the fragments of a child's first toys—a tiny trumpet, bought at some village fair, a baby's rattle, and a broken horse.

Paul Marchmont looked about him—a little puzzled at first; then with a vague dread in his haggard face.

"Mrs. Brown!" he cried, in a loud voice, hurrying across the room towards an inner door as he spoke.

The inner door was opened before Paul could reach it, and a woman appeared; a tall, gaunt-looking woman, with a hard face and bare, brawny arms.

"Where, in Heaven's name, have you been hiding yourself, woman?" Paul cried impatiently. "And where's—your patient?"

"Gone, sir."

"Gone! Where?"

"With her stepmamma, Mrs. Marchmont—not half an hour ago. As it was your wish I should stop behind to clear up, I've done so, sir; but I did think it would have been better for me to have gone with——"

Paul clutched the woman by the arm, and dragged her towards him.

"Are you mad?" he cried, with an oath. "Are you mad, or drunk? Who gave you leave to let that woman go? Who——?"

He couldn't finish the sentence. His throat grew dry, and he gasped for breath; while all the blood in his body seemed to rush into his swollen forehead.

"You sent Mrs. Marchmont to fetch my patient away, sir," exclaimed the woman, looking frightened. "You did, didn't you? She said so!"

"She is a liar; and you are a fool or a cheat. She paid you, I dare say! Can't you speak, woman? Has the person I left in your care, whom you were paid, and paid well, to take care of,—have you let her go? Answer me that."

"I have, sir," the woman faltered,—she was big and brawny, but there was that in Paul Marchmont's face that frightened her notwithstanding,—"seeing as it was your orders."

"That will do," cried Paul Marchmont, holding up his hand and looking at the woman with a ghastly smile; "that will do. You have ruined me; do you hear? You have undone a work that has cost me—O my God! why do I waste my breath in talking to such a creature as this? All my plots, my difficulties, my struggles and victories, my long sleepless nights, my bad dreams,—has it all come to this? Ruin, unutterable ruin, brought upon me by a madwoman!"

He sat down in the chair by the window, and leaned upon the table, scattering the Indian chessmen with his elbow. He did not weep. That relief—terrible relief though it be for a man's breast—was denied him. He sat there with his face covered, moaning aloud. That helpless moan was scarcely like the complaint of a man; it was rather like the hopeless, dreary utterance of a brute's anguish; it sounded like the miserable howling of a beaten cur.

CHAPTER XI.

The sun shone upon Belinda Lawford's wedding-day. The birds were singing in the garden under her window as she opened her lattice and looked out. The word lattice is not a poetical license in this case; for Miss Lawford's chamber was a roomy, old-fashioned apartment at the back of the house, with deep window-seats and diamond-paned casements.

The sun shone, and the roses bloomed in all their summer glory. "'Twas in the time of roses," as gentle-minded Thomas Hood so sweetly sang; surely the time of all others for a bridal morning. The girl looked out into the sunshine with her loose hair falling about her shoulders, and lingered a little looking at the familiar garden, with a half-pensive smile.

"Oh, how often, how often," she said, "I have walked up and down by those laburnums, Letty!" There were two pretty white-curtained bedsteads in the old-fashioned room, and Miss Arundel had shared her friend's apartment for the last week. "How often mamma and I have sat under the dear old cedar, making our poor children's frocks! People say monotonous lives are not happy: mine has been the same thing over and over again; and yet how happy, how happy! And to think that we"—she paused a moment, and the rosy colour in her cheeks deepened by just one shade; it was so sweet to use that simple monosyllable "we" when Edward Arundel was the other half of the pronoun,—"to think that we shall be in Paris to-morrow!"

"Driving in the Bois," exclaimed Miss Arundel; "and dining at the Maison Dorée, or the Café de Paris. Don't dine at Meurice's, Linda; it's dreadfully slow dining at one's hotel. And you'll be a young married woman, and can do anything, you know. If I were a young married woman, I'd ask my husband to take me to the Mabille, just for half an hour, with an old bonnet and a thick veil. I knew a girl whose first-cousin married a cornet in the Guards, and they went to the Mabille one night. Come, Belinda, if you mean to have your back-hair done at all, you'd better sit down at once and let me commence operations."

Miss Arundel had stipulated that, upon this particular morning, she was to dress her friend's hair; and she turned up the frilled sleeves of her white dressing-gown, and set to work in the orthodox manner, spreading a network of shining tresses about Miss Lawford's shoulders, prior to the weaving of elaborate plaits that were to make a crown for the fair young bride. Letitia's tongue went as fast as her fingers; but Belinda was very silent.

She was thinking of the bounteous Providence that had given her the man she loved for her husband. She had been on her knees in the early morning, long before Letitia's awakening, breathing out innocent thanksgiving for the happiness that overflowed her fresh young heart. A woman had need to be country-bred, and to have been reared in the narrow circle of a happy home, to feel as Belinda Lawford felt. Such love as hers is only given to bright and innocent spirits, untarnished even by the knowledge of sin.

Downstairs Edward Arundel was making a wretched pretence of breakfasting *tête-à-tête* with his future father-in-law.

The Major had held his peace as to the unlooked-for visitant of the past night. He had given particular orders that no stranger should be admitted to the house, and that was all. But being of a naturally frank, not to say loquacious disposition, the weight of this secret was a very terrible burden to the honest half-pay soldier. He ate his dry toast uneasily, looking at the door every now and then, in the perpetual expectation of beholding that barrier burst open by mad Olivia Marchmont.

The breakfast was not a very cheerful meal, therefore. I don't suppose any ante-nuptial breakfast ever is very jovial. There was the state banquet—*the* wedding breakfast—to be eaten by-and-by; and Mrs. Lawford, attended by all the females of the establishment, was engaged in putting the last touches to the groups of fruit and confectionery, the pyramids of flowers, and that crowning glory, the wedding-cake.

"Remember the Madeira and still Hock are to go round first, and then the sparkling; and tell Gogram to be particular about the corks, Martha," Mrs. Lawford said to her confidential maid, as she gave a nervous last look at the table. "I was at a breakfast once where a champagne-cork hit the bridegroom on the bridge of his nose at the very moment he rose to return thanks; and being a nervous man, poor fellow,—in point of fact, he was a curate, and the bride was the rector's daughter, with two hundred a year of her own,—it quite overcame him, and he didn't get over it all through the breakfast. And now I must run and put on my bonnet."

There was nothing but putting on bonnets, and pinning lace-shawls, and wild outcries for hair-pins, and interchanging of little feminine services, upon the bedroom floor for the next half-hour.

Major Lawford walked up and down the hall, putting on his white gloves, which were too large for him,—elderly men's white gloves always are too large for them,—and watching the door of the citadel. Olivia must pass over a father's body, the old soldier thought, before she should annoy Belinda on her bridal morning.

By-and-by the carriages came round to the door. The girl bridesmaids came crowding down the stairs, hustling each other's crisped garments, and disputing a little in a sisterly fashion; then Letitia Arundel, with nine rustling flounces of white silk ebbing and flowing and surging about her, and with a pleased simper upon her face; and then followed Mrs. Arundel, stately in silver-grey moire, and Mrs. Lawford, in violet silk—until the hall was a show of bonnets and bouquets and muslin.

And last of all, Belinda Lawford, robed in cloudlike garments of spotless lace, with bridal flowers trembling round her hair, came slowly down the broad old-fashioned staircase, to see her lover loitering in the hall below.

He looked very grave; but he greeted his bride with a tender smile. He loved her, but he could not forget. Even upon this, his wedding-day, the haunting shadow of the past was with him: not to be shaken off.

He did not wait till Belinda reached the bottom of the staircase. There was a sort of ceremonial law to be observed, and he was not to speak to Miss Lawford upon this special morning until he met her in the vestry at Hillingsworth church; so Letitia and Mrs. Arundel hustled the young man into one of the carriages, while Major Lawford ran to receive his daughter at the foot of the stairs.

The Arundel carriage drove off about five minutes before the vehicle that was to convey Major Lawford, Belinda, and as many of the girl bridesmaids as could be squeezed into it without detriment to lace and muslin. The rest went with Mrs. Lawford in the third and last carriage. Hillingsworth church was about three-quarters of a mile from the Grange. It was a pretty irregular old place, lying in a little nook under the shadow of a great yew-tree. Behind the square Norman tower there was a row of poplars, black against the blue summer sky; and between the low gate of the churchyard and the grey, moss-grown porch, there was an avenue of good old elms. The rooks were calling to each other in the topmost branches of the trees as Major Lawford's carriage drew up at the churchyard gate.

Belinda was a great favourite amongst the poor of Hillingsworth parish, and the place had put on a gala-day aspect in honour of her wedding. Garlands of honeysuckle and wild clematis were twined about the stout oaken gate-posts. The school-children were gathered in clusters in the churchyard, with their pinafores full of fresh flowers from shadowy lanes and from prim cottage-gardens,—bright homely blossoms, with the morning dew still upon them.

The rector and his curate were standing in the porch waiting for the coming of the bride; and there were groups of well-dressed people dotted about here and there in the drowsy-sheltered pews near the altar. There were humbler spectators clustered under the low ceiling of the gallery—tradesmen's wives and daughters, radiant with new ribbons, and whispering to one another in delighted anticipation of the show.

Everybody round about the Grange loved pretty, genial Belinda Lawford, and there was universal rejoicing because of her happiness.

The wedding party came out of the vestry presently in appointed order: the bride with her head drooping, and her face hidden by her veil; the bridesmaids' garments making a fluttering noise as they came up the aisle, like the sound of a field of corn faintly stirred by summer breezes.

Then the grave voice of the rector began the service with the brief preliminary exordium; and then, in a tone that grew more solemn with the increasing solemnity of the words, he went on to that awful charge which is addressed especially to the bridegroom and the bride:

"I require and charge you both, as ye will answer at the dreadful day of judgment, when the secrets of all hearts shall be disclosed, that if either of you know any impediment, why ye may not be lawfully joined together in matrimony, ye do now confess it. For be ye well assured——"

The rector read no further; for a woman's voice from out the dusky shadows at the further end of the church cried "Stop!"

There was a sudden silence; people stared at each other with scared faces, and then turned in the direction whence the voice had come. The bride lifted her head for the first time since leaving the vestry, and looked round about her, ashy pale and trembling.

"O Edward, Edward!" she cried, "what is it?"

The rector waited, with his hand still upon the open book. He waited, looking towards the other end of the chancel. He had no need to wait long: a woman, with a black veil thrown back from a white, haggard face, and with dusty garments dragging upon the church-floor, came slowly up the aisle.

Her two hands were clasped upon her breast, and her breath came in gasps, as if she had been running.

"Olivia!" cried Edward Arundel, "what, in Heaven's name——"

But Major Lawford stepped forward, and spoke to the rector.

"Pray let her be got out of the way," he said, in a low voice. "I was warned of this. I was quite prepared for some such disturbance." He sank his voice to a whisper. "*She is mad!*" he said, close in the rector's ear.

The whisper was like whispering in general,—more distinctly audible than the rest of the speech. Olivia Marchmont heard it.

"Mad until to-day," she cried; "but not mad to-day. O Edward Arundel! a hideous wrong has been done by me and through me. Your wife—your wife —"

"My wife! what of her? She—"

"She is alive!" gasped Olivia; "an hour's walk from here. I came on foot. I was tired, and I have been long coming. I thought that I should be in time to stop you before you got to the church; but I am very weak. I ran the last part of the way—"

She dropped her hands upon the altar-rails, and seemed as if she would have fallen. The rector put his arm about her to support her, and she went on:

"I thought I should have spared her this," she said, pointing to Belinda; "but I can't help it. *She* must bear her misery as well as others. It can't be worse for her than it has been for others. She must bear—"

"My wife!" said Edward Arundel; "Mary, my poor sorrowful darling— alive?"

Belinda turned away, and buried her face upon her mother's shoulder. She could have borne anything better than this.

His heart—that supreme treasure, for which she had rendered up thanks to her God—had never been hers after all. A word, a breath, and she was forgotten; his thoughts went back to that other one. There was unutterable joy, there was unspeakable tenderness in his tone, as he spoke of Mary Marchmont, though *she* stood by his side, in all her foolish bridal finery, with her heart newly broken.

"O mother," she cried, "take me away! take me away, before I die!"

Olivia flung herself upon her knees by the altar-rails. Where the pure young bride was to have knelt by her lover's side this wretched sinner cast herself down, sunk far below all common thoughts in the black depth of her despair.

"O my sin, my sin!" she cried, with clasped hands lifted up above her head. "Will God ever forgive my sin? will God ever have pity upon me? Can He pity, can He forgive, such guilt as mine? Even this work of to-day is no atonement to be reckoned against my wickedness. I was jealous of this other woman; I was jealous! Earthly passion was still predominant in this miserable breast."

She rose suddenly, as if this outburst had never been, and laid her hand upon Edward Arundel's arm.

"Come!" she said; "come!"

"To her—to Mary—my wife?"

They had taken Belinda away by this time; but Major Lawford stood looking on. He tried to draw Edward aside; but Olivia's hand upon the young man's arm held him like a vice.

"She is mad," whispered the Major. "Mr. Marchmont came to me last night, and warned me of all this. He told me to be prepared for anything; she has all sorts of delusions. Get her away, if you can, while I go and explain matters to Belinda. Edward, if you have a spark of manly feeling, get this woman away."

But Olivia held the bridegroom's arm with a tightening grasp.

"Come!" she said; "come! Are you turned to stone, Edward Arundel? Is your love worth no more than this? I tell you, your wife, Mary Marchmont, is alive. Let those who doubt me come and see for themselves."

The eager spectators, standing up in the pews or crowding in the narrow aisle, were only too ready to respond to this invitation.

Olivia led her cousin out into the churchyard; she led him to the gate where the carriages were waiting. The crowd flocked after them; and the people outside began to cheer as they came out. That cheer was the signal for which the school-children had waited; and they set to work scattering flowers upon the narrow pathway, before they looked up to see who was coming to trample upon the rosebuds and jessamine, the woodbine and seringa. But they drew back, scared and wondering, as Olivia came along the pathway, sweeping those tender blossoms after her with her trailing black garments, and leading the pale bridegroom by his arm.

She led him to the door of the carriage beside which Major Lawford's gray-haired groom was waiting, with a big white satin favour pinned upon his breast, and a bunch of roses in his button hole. There were favours in the horses' ears, and favours upon the breasts of the Hillingsworth tradespeople who supplied bread and butcher's meat and grocery to the family at the Grange. The bell-ringers up in the church-tower saw the crowd flock out of the porch, and thought the marriage ceremony was over. The jangling bells pealed out upon the hot summer air as Edward stood by the churchyard-gate, with Olivia Marchmont by his side.

"Lend me your carriage," he said to Major Lawford, "and come with me. I must see the end of this. It may be all a delusion; but I must see the end of it. If there is any truth in instinct, I believe that I shall see my wife—alive."

He got into the carriage without further ceremony, and Olivia and Major

Lawford followed him.

"Where is my wife?" the young man asked, letting down the front window as he spoke.

"At Kemberling, at Hester Jobson's."

"Drive to Kemberling," Edward said to the coachman,—"to Kemberling High Street, as fast as you can go."

The man drove away from the churchyard-gate. The humbler spectators, who were restrained by no niceties of social etiquette, hurried after the vehicle, raising white clouds of dust upon the high road with their eager feet. The higher classes lingered about the churchyard, talking to each other and wondering.

Very few people stopped to think of Belinda Lawford. "Let the stricken deer go weep." A stricken deer is a very uninteresting object when there are hounds in full cry hard by, and another deer to be hunted.

"Since when has my wife been at Kemberling?" Edward Arundel asked Olivia, as the carriage drove along the high road between the two villages.

"Since daybreak this morning."

"Where was she before then?"

"At Stony-Stringford Farm."

"And before then?"

"In the pavilion over the boat-house at Marchmont."

"My God! And—"

The young man did not finish his sentence. He put his head out of the window, looking towards Kemberling, and straining his eyes to catch the earliest sight of the straggling village street.

"Faster!" he cried every now and then to the coachman; "faster!"

In little more than half an hour from the time at which it had left the churchyard-gate, the carriage stopped before the little carpenter's shop. Mr. Jobson's doorway was adorned by a painted representation of two very doleful-looking mutes standing at a door; for Hester's husband combined the more aristocratic avocation of undertaker with the homely trade of carpenter and joiner.

Olivia Marchmont got out of the carriage before either of the two men could alight to assist her. Power was the supreme attribute of this woman's mind. Her purpose never faltered; from the moment she had left Marchmont Towers until now, she had known neither rest of body nor wavering of intention.

"Come," she said to Edward Arundel, looking back as she stood upon the threshold of Mr. Jobson's door; "and you too," she added, turning to Major Lawford,—"follow us, and *see* whether I am MAD."

She passed through the shop, and into that prim, smart parlour in which Edward Arundel had lamented his lost wife.

The latticed windows were wide open, and the warm summer sunshine filled the room.

A girl, with loose tresses of hazel-brown hair falling about her face, was sitting on the floor, looking down at a beautiful fair-haired nursling of a twelvemonth old.

The girl was John Marchmont's daughter; the child was Edward Arundel's son. It was *his* childish cry that the young man had heard upon that October night in the pavilion by the water.

"Mary Arundel," said Olivia, in a hard voice, "I give you back your husband."

The young mother got up from the ground with a low cry, tottered forward, and fell into her husband's arms.

"They told me you were dead! They made me believe that you were dead!" she said, and then fainted on the young man's breast. Edward carried her to a sofa and laid her down, white and senseless; and then knelt down beside her, crying over her, and sobbing out inarticulate thanksgiving to the God who had given his lost wife back to him.

"Poor sweet lamb!" murmured Hester Jobson; "she's as weak as a baby; and she's gone through so much a'ready this morning."

It was some time before Edward Arundel raised his head from the pillow upon which his wife's pale face lay, half hidden amid the tangled hair. But when he did look up, he turned to Major Lawford and stretched out his hand.

"Have pity upon me," he said. "I have been the dupe of a villain. Tell your poor child how much I esteem her, how much I regret that—that—we should have loved each other as we have. The instinct of my heart would have kept me true to the past; but it was impossible to know your daughter and not love her. The villain who has brought this sorrow upon us shall pay dearly for his infamy. Go back to your daughter; tell her everything. Tell her what you have seen here. I know her heart, and I know that she will open her arms to this poor ill-used child."

The Major went away very downcast. Hester Jobson bustled about bringing restoratives and pillows, stopping every now and then in an outburst of affection by the slippery horsehair couch on which Mary lay.

Mrs. Jobson had prepared her best bedroom for her beloved visitor, and Edward carried his young wife up to the clean, airy chamber. He went back to the parlour to fetch the child. He carried the fair-haired little one up-stairs in his own arms; but I regret to say that the infant showed an inclination to whimper in his newly-found father's embrace. It is only in the British Drama that newly discovered fathers are greeted with an outburst of ready-made affection. Edward Arundel went back to the sitting-room presently, and sat down, waiting till Hester should bring him fresh tidings of his wife. Olivia Marchmont stood by the window, with her eyes fixed upon Edward.

"Why don't you speak to me?" she said presently. "Can you find no words that are vile enough to express your hatred of me? Is that why you are silent?"

"No, Olivia," answered the young man, calmly. "I am silent, because I have nothing to say to you. Why you have acted as you have acted,—why you have chosen to be the tool of a black-hearted villain,—is an unfathomable mystery to me. I thank God that your conscience was aroused this day, and that you have at least hindered the misery of an innocent girl. But why you have kept my wife hidden from me,—why you have been the accomplice of Paul Marchmont's crime,—is more than I can even attempt to guess."

"Not yet?" said Olivia, looking at him with a strange smile. "Even yet I am a mystery to you?"

"You are, indeed, Olivia."

She turned away from him with a laugh.

"Then I had better remain so till the end," she said, looking out into the garden. But after a moment's silence she turned her head once more towards the young man. "I will speak," she said; "I *will* speak, Edward Arundel. I hope and believe that I have not long to live, and that all my shame and misery, my obstinate wickedness, my guilty passion, will come to an end, like a long feverish dream. O God, have mercy on my waking, and make it brighter than this dreadful sleep! I loved you, Edward Arundel. Ah! you start. Thank God at least for that. I kept my secret well. You don't know what that word 'love' means, do you? You think you love that childish girl yonder, perhaps; but I can tell you that you don't know what love is. *I* know what it is. I have loved. For ten years,—for ten long, dreary, desolate, miserable years, fifty-two weeks in every year, fifty-two Sundays, with long idle hours between the two church services—I have loved you, Edward. Shall I tell you what it is to love? It is to suffer, to hate, yes, to hate even the object of your love, when that love is hopeless; to hate him for the very attributes that have made you love him; to grudge the gifts and graces that have made him dear. It is to hate every creature on whom his eyes look with greater tenderness than they look on you; to watch one face until its familiar lines become a perpetual torment to you, and you cannot sleep because of its eternal presence staring at you in all your dreams. It is to be like some wretched drunkard, who loathes the fiery spirit that is destroying him, body and soul, and yet goes on, madly drinking, till he dies. Love! How many people upon this great earth know the real meaning of that hideous word! I have learnt it until my soul loathes the lesson. They will tell you that I am mad, Edward, and they will tell you something near the truth; but not quite the truth. My madness has been my love. From long ago, when you were little more than a boy—you remember, don't you, the long days at the Rectory? *I* remember every word you ever spoke to me, every sentiment you ever expressed, every look of your changing face—you were the first bright thing that came across my barren life; and I loved you. I married John Marchmont—why, do you think?— because I wanted to make a barrier between you and me. I wanted to make my love for you impossible by making it a sin. So long as my husband lived, I shut your image out of my mind as I would have shut out the Prince of Darkness, if he had come to me in a palpable shape. But since then—oh, I hope I have been mad since then; I hope that God may forgive my sins because I have been mad!"

Her thoughts wandered away to that awful question which had been so lately revived in her mind—Could she be forgiven? Was it within the compass of heavenly mercy to forgive such a sin as hers?

CHAPTER XII.

One of the minor effects of any great shock, any revolution, natural or political, social or domestic, is a singular unconsciousness, or an exaggerated estimate, of the passage of time. Sometimes we fancy that the common functions of the universe have come to a dead stop during the tempest which has shaken our being to its remotest depths. Sometimes, on the other hand, it seems to us that, because we have endured an age of suffering, or half a lifetime of bewildered joy, the terrestrial globe has spun round in time to the quickened throbbing of our passionate hearts, and that all the clocks upon earth have been standing still.

When the sun sank upon the summer's day that was to have been the day of Belinda's bridal, Edward Arundel thought that it was still early in the morning. He wondered at the rosy light all over the western sky, and that great ball of molten gold dropping down below the horizon. He was fain to look at his watch, in order to convince himself that the low light was really the familiar sun, and not some unnatural appearance in the heavens.

And yet, although he wondered at the closing of the day, with a strange inconsistency his mind could scarcely grapple with the idea that only last night he had sat by Belinda Lawford's side, her betrothed husband, and had pondered, Heaven only knows with what sorrowful regret, upon the unknown grave in which his dead wife lay.

"I only knew it this morning," he thought; "I only knew this morning that my young wife still lives, and that I have a son."

He was sitting by the open window in Hester Jobson's best bedroom. He was sitting in an old-fashioned easy-chair, placed between the head of the bed and the open window,—a pure cottage window, with diamond panes of thin greenish glass, and a broad painted ledge, with a great jug of homely garden-flowers standing on it. The young man was sitting by the side of the bed upon which his newly-found wife and son lay asleep; the child's head nestled on his mother's breast, one flushed cheek peeping out of a tangled confusion of hazel-brown and babyish flaxen hair.

The white dimity curtains overshadowed the loving sleepers. The pretty fluffy knotted fringe—neat Hester's handiwork—made fantastical tracery upon the sunlit counterpane. Mary slept with one arm folded round her child, and with her face turned to her husband. She had fallen asleep with her hand clasped in his, after a succession of fainting-fits that had left her terribly prostrate.

Edward Arundel watched that tender picture with a smile of ineffable affection.

"I can understand now why Roman Catholics worship the Virgin Mary," he thought. "I can comprehend the inspiration that guided Raphael's hand when he painted the Madonna de la Chaise. In all the world there is no picture so beautiful. From all the universe he could have chosen no subject more sublime. O my darling wife, given back to me out of the grave, restored to me,—and not alone restored! My little son! my baby-son! whose feeble voice I heard that dark October night. To think that I was so wretched a dupe! to think that my dull ears could hear that sound, and no instinct rise up in my heart to reveal the presence of my child! I was so near them, not once, but several times,—so near, and I never knew—I never guessed!"

He clenched his fists involuntarily at the remembrance of those purposeless visits to the lonely boat-house. His young wife was restored to him. But nothing could wipe away the long interval of agony in which he and she had been the dupe of a villanous trickster and a jealous woman. Nothing could give back the first year of that baby's life,—that year which should have been one long holiday of love and rejoicing. Upon what a dreary world those innocent eyes had opened, when they should have looked only upon sunshine and flowers, and the tender light of a loving father's smile!

"O my darling, my darling!" the young husband thought, as he looked at his wife's wan face, upon which the evidence of all that past agony was only too painfully visible,—"how bitterly we two have suffered! But how much more terrible must have been your suffering than mine, my poor gentle darling, my broken lily!"

In his rapture at finding the wife he had mourned as dead, the young man had for a time almost forgotten the villanous plotter who had kept her hidden from him. But now, as he sat quietly by the bed upon which Mary and her baby lay, he had leisure to think of Paul Marchmont.

What was he to do with that man? What vengeance could he wreak upon the head of that wretch who, for nearly two years, had condemned an innocent girl to cruel suffering and shame? To shame; for Edward knew now that one of the most bitter tortures which Paul Marchmont had inflicted upon his cousin had been his pretended disbelief in her marriage.

"What can I do to him?" the young man asked himself. "*What* can I do to him? There is no personal chastisement worse than that which he has endured already at my hands. The scoundrel! the heartless villain! the false, cold-blooded cur! What can I do to him? I can only repeat that shameful degradation, and I *will* repeat it. This time he shall howl under the lash like some beaten hound. This time I will drag him through the village-street, and let every idle gossip in Kemberling see how a scoundrel writhes under an honest man's whip. I will—"

Edward Arundel's wife woke while he was thinking what chastisement he should inflict upon her deadly foe; and the baby opened his round innocent blue eyes in the next moment, and sat up, staring at his new parent.

Mr. Arundel took the child in his arms, and held him very tenderly, though perhaps rather awkwardly. The baby's round eyes opened wider at sight of those golden absurdities dangling at his father's watch-chain, and the little pudgy hands began to play with the big man's lockets and seals.

"He comes to me, you see, Mary!" Edward said, with naïve wonder.

And then he turned the baby's face towards him, and tenderly contemplated the bright surprised blue eyes, the tiny dimples, the soft moulded chin. I don't know whether fatherly vanity prompted the fancy, but Edward Arundel certainly did believe that he saw some faint reflection of his own features in that pink and white baby-face; a shadowy resemblance, like a tremulous image looking up out of a river. But while Edward was half-thinking this, half-wondering whether there could be any likeness to him in that infant countenance, Mary settled the question with womanly decision.

"Isn't he like you, Edward?" she whispered. "It was only for his sake that I bore my life all through that miserable time; and I don't think I could have lived even for him, if he hadn't been so like you. I used to look at his face sometimes for hours and hours together, crying over him, and thinking of you. I don't think I ever cried except when he was in my arms. Then something seemed to soften my heart, and the tears came to my eyes. I was very, very, very ill, for a long time before my baby was born; and I didn't know how the time went, or where I was. I used to fancy sometimes I was back in Oakley Street, and that papa was alive again, and that we were quite happy together, except for some heavy hammer that was always beating, beating, beating upon both our heads, and the dreadful sound of the river rushing down the street under our windows. I heard Mr. Weston tell his wife that it was a miracle I lived through that time."

Hester Jobson came in presently with a tea-tray, that made itself heard, by a jingling of teaspoons and rattling of cups and saucers, all the way up the narrow staircase.

The friendly carpenter's wife had produced her best china and her silver teapot,—an heirloom inherited from a wealthy maiden aunt of her husband's. She had been busy all the afternoon, preparing that elegant little collation of cake and fruit which accompanied the tea-tray; and she spread the lavender-scented table-cloth, and arranged the cups and saucers, the plates and dishes, with mingled pride and delight.

But she had to endure a terrible disappointment by-and-by; for neither of her guests was in a condition to do justice to her hospitality. Mary got up and sat in the roomy easy-chair, propped up with pillows. Her pensive eyes kept a loving watch upon the face of her husband, turned towards her own, and slightly crimsoned by that rosy flush fading out in the western sky. She sat up and sipped a cup of tea; and in that lovely summer twilight, with the scent of the flowers blowing in through the open window, and a stupid moth doing his best to beat out his brains against one of the diamond panes in the lattice, the tortured heart, for the first time since the ruthless close of that brief honeymoon, felt the heavenly delight of repose.

"O Edward!" murmured the young wife, "how strange it seems to be happy!"

He was at her feet, half-kneeling, half-sitting on a hassock of Hester's handiwork, with both his wife's hands clasped in his, and his head leaning upon the arm of her chair. Hester Jobson had carried off the baby, and these two were quite alone, all in all to each other, with a cruel gap of two years to be bridged over by sorrowful memories, by tender words of consolation. They were alone, and they could talk quite freely now, without fear of interruption; for although in purity and beauty an infant is first cousin to the angels, and although I most heartily concur in all that Mr. Bennett and Mr. Buchanan can say or sing about the species, still it must be owned that a baby *is* rather a hindrance to conversation, and that a man's eloquence does not flow quite so smoothly when he has to stop every now and then to rescue his infant son from the imminent peril of strangulation, caused by a futile attempt at swallowing one of his own fists.

Mary and Edward were alone; they were together once more, as they had been by the trout-stream in the Winchester meadows. A curtain had fallen upon all the wreck and ruin of the past, and they could hear the soft, mysterious music that was to be the prelude of a new act in life's drama.

"I shall try to forget all that time," Mary said presently; "I shall try to forget it, Edward. I think the very memory of it would kill me, if it was to come back perpetually in the midst of my joy, as it does now, even now, when I am so happy—so happy that I dare not speak of my happiness."

She stopped, and her face drooped upon her husband's clustering hair.

"You are crying, Mary!"

"Yes, dear. There is something painful in happiness when it comes after such suffering."

The young man lifted his head, and looked in his wife's face. How deathly pale it was, even in that shadowy twilight; how worn and haggard and wasted since it had smiled at him in his brief honeymoon. Yes, joy is painful when it comes after a long continuance of suffering; it is painful because we have become sceptical by reason of the endurance of such anguish. We have lost the power to believe in happiness. It comes, the bright stranger; but we shrink appalled from its beauty, lest, after all, it should be nothing but a phantom.

Heaven knows how anxiously Edward Arundel looked at his wife's altered face. Her eyes shone upon him with the holy light of love. She smiled at him with a tender, reassuring smile; but it seemed to him that there was something almost supernal in the brightness of that white, wasted face; something that reminded him of the countenance of a martyr who has ceased to suffer the anguish of death in a foretaste of the joys of Heaven.

"Mary," he said, presently, "tell me every cruelty that Paul Marchmont or his tools inflicted upon you; tell me everything, and I will never speak of our miserable separation again. I will only punish the cause of it," he added, in an undertone. "Tell me, dear. It will be painful for you to speak of it; but it will be only once. There are some things I must know. Remember, darling, that you are in my arms now, and that nothing but death can ever again part us."

The young man had his arms round his wife. He felt, rather than heard, a low plaintive sigh as he spoke those last words.

"Nothing but death, Edward; nothing but death," Mary said, in a solemn whisper. "Death would not come to me when I was very miserable. I used to pray that I might die, and the baby too; for I could not have borne to leave him behind. I thought that we might both be buried with you, Edward. I have dreamt sometimes that I was lying by your side in a tomb, and I have stretched out my dead hand to clasp yours. I used to beg and entreat them to let me be buried with you when I died; for I believed that you were dead, Edward. I believed it most firmly. I had not even one lingering hope that you were alive. If I had felt such a hope, no power upon earth would have kept me prisoner."

"The wretches!" muttered Edward between his set teeth; "the dastardly wretches! the foul liars!"

"Don't, Edward; don't, darling. There is a pain in my heart when I hear you speak like that. I know how wicked they have been; how cruel—how cruel. I look back at all my suffering as if it were some one else who suffered; for now that you are with me I cannot believe that miserable, lonely, despairing creature was really me, the same creature whose head now rests upon your shoulder, whose breath is mixed with yours. I look back and see all my past misery, and I cannot forgive them, Edward; I am very wicked, for I cannot forgive my cousin Paul and his sister—yet. But I don't want you to speak of them; I only want you to love me; I only want you to smile at me, and tell me again and again and again that nothing can part us now—but death."

She paused for a few moments, exhausted by having spoken so long. Her head lay upon her husband's shoulder, and she clung a little closer to him, with a slight shiver.

"What is the matter, darling?"

"I feel as if it couldn't be real."

"What, dear?"

"The present—all this joy. Edward, is it real? Is it—is it? Or am I only dreaming? Shall I wake presently and feel the cold air blowing in at the window, and see the moonlight on the wainscot at Stony Stringford? Is it all real?"

"It is, my precious one. As real as the mercy of God, who will give you compensation for all you have suffered; as real as God's vengeance, which will fall most heavily upon your persecutors. And now, darling, tell me,—tell me all. I must know the story of these two miserable years during which I have mourned for my lost love."

Mr. Arundel forgot to mention that during those two miserable years he had engaged himself to become the husband of another woman. But perhaps, even when he is best and truest, a man is always just a shade behind a woman in the matter of constancy.

"When you left me in Hampshire, Edward, I was very, very miserable," Mary began, in a low voice; "but I knew that it was selfish and wicked of me to think only of myself. I tried to think of your poor father, who was ill and suffering; and I prayed for him, and hoped that he would recover, and that you would come back to me very soon. The people at the inn were very kind to me. I sat at the window from morning till night upon the day after you left me, and upon the day after that; for I was so foolish as to fancy, every time I heard the sound of horses' hoofs or carriage-wheels upon the high-road, that you were coming back to me, and that all my grief was over. I sat at the window and watched the road till I knew the shape of every tree and housetop, every ragged branch of the hawthorn-bushes in the hedge. At last—it was the third day after you went away—I heard carriage-wheels, that slackened as they came to the inn. A fly stopped at the door, and oh, Edward, I did not wait to see who was in it,—I never imagined the possibility of its bringing anybody but you. I ran down-stairs, with my heart beating so that I could hardly breathe; and I scarcely felt the stairs under my feet. But when I got to the door—O my love, my love!—I cannot bear to think of it; I cannot endure the recollection of it—"

She stopped, gasping for breath, and clinging to her husband; and then, with an effort, went on again:

"Yes; I will tell you, dear; I must tell you. My cousin Paul and my stepmother were standing in the little hall at the foot of the stairs. I think I fainted in my stepmother's arms; and when my consciousness came back, I was in our sitting-room,—the pretty rustic room, Edward, in which you and I had been so happy together.

"I must not stop to tell you everything. It would take me so long to speak of all that happened in that miserable time. I knew that something must be wrong, from my cousin Paul's manner; but neither he nor my stepmother would tell me what it was. I asked them if you were dead; but they said, 'No, you were not dead.' Still I could see that something dreadful had happened. But by-and-by, by accident, I saw your name in a newspaper that was lying on the table with Paul's hat and gloves. I saw the description of an accident on the railway, by which I knew you had travelled. My heart sank at once, and I think I guessed all that had happened. I read your name amongst those of the people who had been dangerously hurt. Paul shook his head when I asked him if there was any hope.

"They brought me back here. I scarcely know how I came, how I endured all that misery. I implored them to let me come to you, again and again, on my knees at their feet. But neither of them would listen to me. It was impossible, Paul said. He always seemed very, very kind to me; always spoke softly; always told me that he pitied me, and was sorry for me. But though my stepmother looked sternly at me, and spoke, as she always used to speak, in a harsh, cold voice, I sometimes think she might have given way at last and let me come to you, but for him—but for my cousin Paul. He could look at me with a smile upon his face when I was almost mad with my misery; and he never wavered; he never hesitated.

"So they took me back to the Towers. I let them take me; for I scarcely felt my sorrow any longer. I only felt tired; oh, so dreadfully tired; and I wanted to lie down upon the ground in some quiet place, where no one could come near me. I thought that I was dying. I believe I was very ill when we got back to the Towers. My stepmother and Barbara Simmons watched by my bedside, day after day, night after night. Sometimes I knew them; sometimes I had all sorts of fancies. And often—ah, how often, darling!—I thought that you were with me. My cousin Paul came every day, and stood by my bedside. I can't tell you how hateful it was to me to have him there. He used to come into the room as silently as if he had been walking upon snow; but however noiselessly he came, however fast asleep I was when he entered the room, I always knew that he was there, standing by my bedside, smiling at me. I always woke with a shuddering horror thrilling through my veins, as if a rat had run across my face.

"By-and-by, when the delirium was quite gone, I felt ashamed of myself for this. It seemed so wicked to feel this unreasonable antipathy to my dear father's cousin; but he had brought me bad news of you, Edward, and it was scarcely strange that I should hate him. One day he sat down by my bedside, when I was getting better, and was strong enough to talk. There was no one besides ourselves in the room, except my stepmother, and she was standing at the window, with her head turned away from us, looking out. My cousin Paul sat down by the bedside, and began to talk to me in that gentle, compassionate way that used to torture me and irritate me in spite of myself.

"He asked me what had happened to me after my leaving the Towers on the day after the ball.

"I told him everything, Edward—about your coming to me in Oakley Street; about our marriage. But, oh, my darling, my husband, he wouldn't believe me; he wouldn't believe. Nothing that I could say would make him believe me. Though I swore to him again and again—by my dead father in heaven, as I hoped for the mercy of my God—that I had spoken the truth, and the truth only, he wouldn't believe me; he wouldn't believe. He shook his head, and said he scarcely wondered I should try to deceive him; that it was a very sad story, a very miserable and shameful story, and my attempted falsehood was little more than natural.

"And then he spoke against you, Edward—against you. He talked of my childish ignorance, my confiding love, and your villany. O Edward, he said such shameful things; such shameful, horrible things! You had plotted to become master of my fortune; to get me into your power, because of my money; and you had not married me. You had *not* married me; he persisted in saying that.

"I was delirious again after this; almost mad, I think. All through the delirium I kept telling my cousin Paul of our marriage. Though he was very seldom in the room, I constantly thought that he was there, and told him the same thing —the same thing—till my brain was on fire. I don't know how long it lasted. I know that, once in the middle of the night, I saw my stepmother lying upon the ground, sobbing aloud and crying out about her wickedness; crying out that God would never forgive her sin.

"I got better at last, and then I went downstairs; and I used to sit sometimes in poor papa's study. The blind was always down, and none of the servants, except Barbara Simmons, ever came into the room. My cousin Paul did not live at the Towers; but he came there every day, and often stayed there all day. He seemed the master of the house. My stepmother obeyed him in everything, and consulted him about everything.

"Sometimes Mrs. Weston came. She was like her brother. She always smiled at me with a grave compassionate smile, just like his; and she always seemed to pity me. But she wouldn't believe in my marriage. She spoke cruelly about you, Edward; cruelly, but in soft words, that seemed only spoken out of compassion for me. No one would believe in my marriage.

"No stranger was allowed to see me. I was never suffered to go out. They treated me as if I was some shameful creature, who must be hidden away from the sight of the world.

"One day I entreated my cousin Paul to go to London and see Mrs. Pimpernel. She would be able to tell him of our marriage. I had forgotten the name of the clergyman who married us, and the church at which we were married. And I could not tell Paul those; but I gave him Mrs. Pimpernel's address. And I wrote to her, begging her to tell my cousin, all about my marriage; and I gave him the note unsealed.

"He went to London about a week afterwards; and when he came back, he brought me my note. He had been to Oakley Street, he said; but Mrs. Pimpernel had left the neighbourhood, and no one knew where she was gone."

"A lie! a villanous lie!" muttered Edward Arundel. "Oh, the scoundrel! the infernal scoundrel!"

"No words would ever tell the misery of that time; the bitter anguish; the unendurable suspense. When I asked them about you, they would tell me nothing. Sometimes I thought that you had forgotten me; that you had only married me out of pity for my loneliness; and that you were glad to be freed from me. Oh, forgive me, Edward, for that wicked thought; but I was so very miserable, so utterly desolate. At other times I fancied that you were very ill, helpless, and unable to come to me. I dared not think that you were dead. I put away that thought from me with all my might; but it haunted me day and night. It was with me always like a ghost. I tried to shut it away from my sight; but I knew that it was there.

"The days were all alike,—long, dreary, and desolate; so I scarcely know how the time went. My stepmother brought me religious books, and told me to read them; but they were hard, difficult books, and I couldn't find one word of comfort in them. They must have been written to frighten very obstinate and wicked people, I think. The only book that ever gave me any comfort, was that dear Book I used to read to papa on a Sunday evening in Oakley Street. I read that, Edward, in those miserable days; I read the story of the widow's only son who was raised up from the dead because his mother was so wretched without him. I read that sweet, tender story again and again, until I used to see the funeral train, the pale, still face upon the bier, the white, uplifted hand, and that sublime and lovely countenance, whose image always comes to us when we are most miserable, the tremulous light upon the golden hair, and in the distance the glimmering columns of white temples, the palm-trees standing out against the purple Eastern sky. I thought that He who raised up a miserable woman's son chiefly because he was her only son, and she was desolate without him, would have more pity upon me than the God in Olivia's books: and I prayed to Him, Edward, night and day, imploring Him to bring you back to me.

"I don't know what day it was, except that it was autumn, and the dead leaves were blowing about in the quadrangle, when my stepmother sent for me one afternoon to my room, where I was sitting, not reading, not even thinking— only sitting with my head upon my hands, staring stupidly out at the drifting leaves and the gray, cold sky. My stepmother was in papa's study; and I was to go to her there. I went, and found her standing there, with a letter crumpled up in her clenched hand, and a slip of newspaper lying on the table before her. She was as white as death, and she was trembling violently from head to foot.

"'See,' she said, pointing to the paper; 'your lover is dead. But for you he would have received the letter that told him of his father's illness upon an earlier day; he would have gone to Devonshire by a different train. It was by your doing that he travelled when he did. If this is true, and he is dead, his blood be upon your head; his blood be upon your head!'

"I think her cruel words were almost exactly those. I did not hope for a minute that those horrible lines in the newspaper were false. I thought they must be true, and I was mad, Edward—I was mad; for utter despair came to me with the knowledge of your death. I went to my own room, and put on my bonnet and shawl; and then I went out of the house, down into that dreary wood, and along the narrow pathway by the river-side. I wanted to drown myself; but the sight of the black water filled me with a shuddering horror. I was frightened, Edward; and I went on by the river, scarcely knowing where I was going, until it was quite dark; and I was tired, and sat down upon the damp ground by the brink of the river, all amongst the broad green flags and the wet rushes. I sat there for hours, and I saw the stars shining feebly in a dark sky. I think I was delirious, for sometimes I knew that I was there by the water side, and then the next minute I thought that I was in my bedroom at the Towers; sometimes I fancied that I was with you in the meadows near Winchester, and the sun was shining, and you were sitting by my side, and I could see your float dancing up and down in the sunlit water. At last, after I had been there a very, very long time, two people came with a lantern, a man and a woman; and I heard a startled voice say, 'Here she is; here, lying on the ground!' And then another voice, a woman's voice, very low and frightened, said, 'Alive!' And then two people lifted me up; the man carried me in his arms, and the woman took the lantern. I couldn't speak to them; but I knew that they were my cousin Paul and his sister, Mrs. Weston. I remember being carried some distance in Paul's arms; and then I think I must have fainted away, for I can recollect nothing more until I woke up one day and found myself lying in a bed in the pavilion over the boat-house, with Mr. Weston watching by my bedside.

"I don't know how the time passed; I only know that it seemed endless. I think my illness was rheumatic fever, caught by lying on the damp ground nearly all that night when I ran away from the Towers. A long time went by— there was frost and snow. I saw the river once out of the window when I was lifted out of bed for an hour or two, and it was frozen; and once at midnight I heard the Kemberling church-bells ringing in the New Year. I was very ill, but I had no doctor; and all that time I saw no one but my cousin Paul, and Lavinia Weston, and a servant called Betsy, a rough country girl, who took care of me when my cousins were away. They were kind to me, and took great care of me."

"You did not see Olivia, then, all this time?" Edward asked eagerly.

"No; I did not see my stepmother till some time after the New Year began. She came in suddenly one evening, when Mrs. Weston was with me, and at first she seemed frightened at seeing me. She spoke to me kindly afterwards, but in a strange, terror-stricken voice; and she laid her head down upon the counterpane of the bed, and sobbed aloud; and then Paul took her away, and spoke to her cruelly, very cruelly—taunting her with her love for you. I never understood till then why she hated me: but I pitied her after that; yes, Edward, miserable as I was, I pitied her, because you had never loved her. In all my wretchedness I was happier than her; for you had loved me, Edward—you had loved me!"

Mary lifted her face to her husband's lips, and those dear lips were pressed tenderly upon her pale forehead.

"O my love, my love!" the young man murmured; "my poor suffering angel! Can God ever forgive these people for their cruelty to you? But, my darling, why did you make no effort to escape?"

"I was too ill to move; I believed that I was dying."

"But afterwards, darling, when you were better, stronger,—did you make no effort then to escape from your persecutors?"

Mary shook her head mournfully.

"Why should I try to escape from them?" she said. "What was there for me beyond that place? It was as well for me to be there as anywhere else. I thought you were dead, Edward; I thought you were dead, and life held nothing more for me. I could do nothing but wait till He who raised the widow's son should have pity upon me, and take me to the heaven where I thought you and papa had gone before me. I didn't want to go away from those dreary rooms over the boat-house. What did it matter to me whether I was there or at Marchmont Towers? I thought you were dead, and all the glories and grandeurs of the world were nothing to me. Nobody ill-treated me; I was let alone. Mrs. Weston told me that it was for my own sake they kept me hidden from everybody about the Towers. I was a poor disgraced girl, she told me; and it was best for me to stop quietly in the pavilion till people had got tired of talking of me, and then my cousin Paul would take me away to the Continent, where no one would know who I was. She told me that the honour of my father's name, and of my family altogether, would be saved by this means. I replied that I had brought no dishonour on my dear father's name; but she only shook her head mournfully, and I was too weak to dispute with her. What did it matter? I thought you were dead, and that the world was finished for me. I sat day after day by the window; not looking out, for there was a Venetian blind that my cousin Paul had nailed down to the window-sill, and I could only see glimpses of the water through the long, narrow openings between the laths. I used to sit there listening to the moaning of the wind amongst the trees, or the sounds of horses' feet upon the towing-path, or the rain dripping into the river upon wet days. I think that even in my deepest misery God was good to me, for my mind sank into a dull apathy, and I seemed to lose even the capacity of suffering.

"One day,—one day in March, when the wind was howling, and the smoke blew down the narrow chimney and filled the room,—Mrs. Weston brought her husband, and he talked to me a little, and then talked to his wife in whispers. He seemed terribly frightened, and he trembled all the time, and kept saying, 'Poor thing; poor young woman!' but his wife was cross to him, and wouldn't let him stop long in the room. After that, Mr. Weston came very often, always with Lavinia, who seemed cleverer than he was, even as a doctor; for she dictated to him, and ordered him about in everything. Then, by-and-by, when the birds were singing, and the warm sunshine came into the room, my baby was born, Edward; my baby was born. I thought that God, who raised the widow's son, had heard my prayer, and had raised you up from the dead; for the baby's eyes were like yours, and I used to think sometimes that your soul was looking out of them and comforting me.

"Do you remember that poor foolish German woman who believed that the spirit of a dead king came to her in the shape of a blackbird? She was not a good woman, I know, dear; but she must have loved the king very truly, or she never could have believed anything so foolish. I don't believe in people's love when they love 'wisely,' Edward: the truest love is that which loves 'too well.'

"From the time of my baby's birth everything was changed. I was more miserable, perhaps, because that dull, dead apathy cleared away, and my memory came back, and I thought of you, dear, and cried over my little angel's face as he slept. But I wasn't alone any longer. The world seemed narrowed into the little circle round my darling's cradle. I don't think he is like other babies, Edward. I think he has known of my sorrow from the very first, and has tried in his mute way to comfort me. The God who worked so many miracles, all separate tokens of His love and tenderness and pity for the sorrows of mankind, could easily make my baby different from other children, for a wretched mother's consolation.

"In the autumn after my darling's birth, Paul and his sister came for me one night, and took me away from the pavilion by the water to a deserted farmhouse, where there was a woman to wait upon me and take care of me. She was not unkind to me, but she was rather neglectful of me. I did not mind that, for I wanted nothing except to be alone with my precious boy—your son, Edward; your son. The woman let me walk in the garden sometimes. It was a neglected garden, but there were bright flowers growing wild, and when the spring came again my pet used to lie on the grass and play with the buttercups and daisies that I threw into his lap; and I think we were both of us happier and better than we had been in those two close rooms over the boat-house.

"I have told you all now, Edward, all except what happened this morning, when my stepmother and Hester Jobson came into my room in the early daybreak, and told me that I had been deceived, and that you were alive. My stepmother threw herself upon her knees at my feet, and asked me to forgive her, for she was a miserable sinner, she said, who had been abandoned by God; and I forgave her, Edward, and kissed her; and you must forgive her too, dear, for I know that she has been very, very wretched. And she took the baby in her arms, and kissed him,—oh, so passionately!—and cried over him. And then they brought me here in Mr. Jobson's cart, for Mr. Jobson was with them, and Hester held me in her arms all the time. And then, darling, then after a long time you came to me."

Edward put his arms round his wife, and kissed her once more. "We will never speak of this again, darling," he said. "I know all now; I understand it all. I will never again distress you by speaking of your cruel wrongs."

"And you will forgive Olivia, dear?"

"Yes, my pet, I will forgive—Olivia."

He said no more, for there was a footstep on the stair, and a glimmer of light shone through the crevices of the door. Hester Jobson came into the room with a pair of lighted wax-candles, in white crockery-ware candlesticks. But Hester was not alone; close behind her came a lady in a rustling silk gown, a tall matronly lady, who cried out,—

"Where is she, Edward? Where is she? Let me see this poor ill-used child."

It was Mrs. Arundel, who had come to Kemberling to see her newly-found daughter-in-law.

"Oh, my dear mother," cried the young man, "how good of you to come! Now, Mary, you need never again know what it is to want a protector, a tender womanly protector, who will shelter you from every harm."

Mary got up and went to Mrs. Arundel, who opened her arms to receive her son's young wife. But before she folded Mary to her friendly breast, she took the girl's two hands in hers, and looked earnestly at her pale, wasted face.

She gave a long sigh as she contemplated those wan features, the shining light in the eyes, that looked unnaturally large by reason of the girl's hollow cheeks.

"Oh, my dear," cried Mrs. Arundel, "my poor long-suffering child, how cruelly they have treated you!"

Edward looked at his mother, frightened by the earnestness of her manner; but she smiled at him with a bright, reassuring look.

"I shall take you home to Dangerfield with me, my poor love," she said to Mary; "and I shall nurse you, and make you as plump as a partridge, my poor wasted pet. And I'll be a mother to you, my motherless child. Oh, to think that there should be any wretch vile enough to—But I won't agitate you, my dear. I'll take you away from this bleak horrid county by the first train to-morrow morning, and you shall sleep to-morrow night in the blue bedroom at Dangerfield, with the roses and myrtles waving against your window; and Edward shall go with us, and you shan't come back here till you are well and strong; and you'll try and love me, won't you, dear? And, oh, Edward, I've seen the boy! and he's a *superb* creature, the very *image* of what you were at a twelvemonth old; and he came to me, and smiled at me, almost as if he knew

I was his grandmother; and he has got FIVE teeth, but I'm *sorry* to tell you he's cutting them crossways, the top first instead of the bottom, Hester says."

"And Belinda, mother dear?" Edward said presently, in a grave undertone.

"Belinda is an angel," Mrs. Arundel answered, quite as gravely. "She has been in her own room all day, and no one has seen her but her mother; but she came down to the hall as I was leaving the house this evening, and said to me, 'Dear Mrs. Arundel, tell him that he must not think I am so selfish as to be sorry for what has happened. Tell him that I am very glad to think his young wife has been saved.' She put her hand up to my lips to stop my speaking, and then went back again to her room; and if that isn't acting like an angel, I don't know what is."

CHAPTER XIII.

Paul Marchmont did not leave Stony-Stringford Farmhouse till dusk upon that bright summer's day; and the friendly twilight is slow to come in the early days of July, however a man may loathe the sunshine. Paul Marchmont stopped at the deserted farmhouse, wandering in and out of the empty rooms, strolling listlessly about the neglected garden, or coming to a dead stop sometimes, and standing stock-still for ten minutes at a time, staring at the wall before him, and counting the slimy traces of the snails upon the branches of a plum-tree, or the flies in a spider's web. Paul Marchmont was afraid to leave that lonely farmhouse. He was afraid as yet. He scarcely knew what he feared, for a kind of stupor had succeeded the violent emotions of the past few hours; and the time slipped by him, and his brain grew bewildered when he tried to realise his position.

It was very difficult for him to do this. The calamity that had come upon him was a calamity that he had never anticipated. He was a clever man, and he had put his trust in his own cleverness. He had never expected to be *found out.*

Until this hour everything had been in his favour. His dupes and victims had played into his hands. Mary's grief, which had rendered her a passive creature, utterly indifferent to her own fate,—her peculiar education, which had taught her everything except knowledge of the world in which she was to live,—had enabled Paul Marchmont to carry out a scheme so infamous and daring that it was beyond the suspicion of honest men, almost too base for the comprehension of ordinary villains.

He had never expected to be found out. All his plans had been deliberately and carefully prepared. Immediately after Edward's marriage and safe departure for the Continent, Paul had intended to convey Mary and the child, with the grim attendant whom he had engaged for them, far away, to one of the remotest villages in Wales.

Alone he would have done this; travelling by night, and trusting no one; for the hired attendant knew nothing of Mary's real position. She had been told that the girl was a poor relation of Paul's, and that her story was a very sorrowful one. If the poor creature had strange fancies and delusions, it was no more than might be expected; for she had suffered enough to turn a stronger brain than her own. Everything had been arranged, and so cleverly arranged, that Mary and the child would disappear after dusk one summer's evening, and not even Lavinia Weston would be told whither they had gone.

Paul had never expected to be found out. But he had least of all expected betrayal from the quarter whence it had come. He had made Olivia his tool; but he had acted cautiously even with her. He had confided nothing to her; and although she had suspected some foul play in the matter of Mary's disappearance, she had been certain of nothing. She had uttered no falsehood when she swore to Edward Arundel that she did not know where his wife was. But for her accidental discovery of the secret of the pavilion, she would never have known of Mary's existence after that October afternoon on which the girl left Marchmont Towers.

But here Paul had been betrayed by the carelessness of the hired girl who acted as Mary Arundel's gaoler and attendant. It was Olivia's habit to wander often in that dreary wood by the water during the winter in which Mary was kept prisoner in the pavilion over the boat-house. Lavinia Weston and Paul Marchmont spent each of them a great deal of their time in the pavilion; but they could not be always on guard there. There was the world to be hoodwinked; and the surgeon's wife had to perform all her duties as a matron before the face of Kemberling, and had to give some plausible account of her frequent visits to the boat-house. Paul liked the place for his painting, Mrs. Weston informed her friends; and he was *so* enthusiastic in his love of art, that it was really a pleasure to participate in his enthusiasm; so she liked to sit with him, and talk to him or read to him while he painted. This explanation was quite enough for Kemberling; and Mrs. Weston went to the pavilion at Marchmont Towers three or four times a week without causing any scandal thereby.

But however well you may manage things yourself, it is not always easy to secure the careful co-operation of the people you employ. Betsy Murrel was a stupid, narrow-minded young person, who was very safe so far as regarded the possibility of any sympathy with, or compassion for, Mary Arundel arising in her stolid nature; but the stupid stolidity which made her safe in one way rendered her dangerous in another. One day, while Mrs. Weston was with the hapless young prisoner, Miss Murrel went out upon the water-side to converse with a good-looking young bargeman, who was a connexion of her family, and perhaps an admirer of the young lady herself; and the door of the painting-room being left wide open, Olivia Marchmont wandered listlessly into the pavilion—there was a dismal fascination for her in that spot, on which she had heard Edward Arundel declare his love for John Marchmont's daughter—and heard Mary's voice in the chamber at the top of the stone steps.

This was how Olivia had surprised Paul's secret; and from that hour it had been the artist's business to rule this woman by the only weapon which he possessed against her,—her own secret, her own weak folly, her mad love of Edward Arundel and jealous hatred of the woman whom he had loved. This weapon was a very powerful one, and Paul used it unsparingly.

When the woman who, for seven-and-twenty years of her life, had lived without sin; who from the hour in which she had been old enough to know right from wrong, until Edward Arundel's second return from India, had sternly done her duty,—when this woman, who little by little had slipped away from her high standing-point and sunk down into a morass of sin; when this woman remonstrated with Mr. Marchmont, he turned upon her and lashed her with the scourge of her own folly.

"You come and upbraid me," he said, "and you call me villain and arch-traitor, and say that you cannot abide this, your sin; and that your guilt, in keeping our secret, cries to you in the dead hours of the night; and you call upon me to undo what I have done, and to restore Mary Marchmont to her rights. Do you remember what her highest right is? Do you remember that which I must restore to her when I give her back this house and the income that goes along with it? If I restore Marchmont Towers, I must restore to her *Edward Arundel's love!* You have forgotten that, perhaps. If she ever re-enters this house, she will come back to it leaning on his arm. You will see them together—you will hear of their happiness; and do you think that *he* will ever forgive you for your part of the conspiracy? Yes, it is a conspiracy, if you like; if you are not afraid to call it by a hard name, why should I fear to do so? Will he ever forgive you, do you think, when he knows that his young wife has been the victim of a senseless, vicious love? Yes, Olivia Marchmont; any love is vicious which is given unsought, and is so strong a passion, so blind and unreasoning a folly, that honour, mercy, truth, and Christianity are trampled down before it. How will you endure Edward Arundel's contempt for you? How will you tolerate his love for Mary, multiplied twentyfold by all this romantic business of separation and persecution?

"You talk to me of my sin. Who was it who first sinned? Who was it who drove Mary Marchmont from this house,—not once only, but twice, by her cruelty? Who was it who persecuted her and tortured her day by day and hour by hour, not openly, not with an uplifted hand or blows that could be warded off, but by cruel hints and inuendoes, by unwomanly sneers and hellish taunts? Look into your heart, Olivia Marchmont; and when you make atonement for your sin, I will make restitution for mine. In the meantime, if this business is painful to you, the way lies open before you: go and take Edward Arundel to the pavilion yonder, and give him back his wife; give the lie to all your past life, and restore these devoted young lovers to each other's arms."

This weapon never failed in its effect. Olivia Marchmont might loathe herself, and her sin, and her life, which was made hideous to her because of her sin; but she *could* not bring herself to restore Mary to her lover-husband; she could not tolerate the idea of their happiness. Every night she grovelled on her knees, and swore to her offended God that she would do this thing, she would render this sacrifice of atonement; but every morning, when her weary eyes opened on the hateful sunlight, she cried, "Not to-day—not to-day."

Again and again, during Edward Arundel's residence at Kemberling Retreat, she had set out from Marchmont Towers with the intention of revealing to him the place where his young wife was hidden; but, again and again, she had turned back and left her work undone. She *could* not—she could not. In the dead of the night, under pouring rain, with the bleak winds of winter blowing in her face, she had set out upon that unfinished journey, only to stop midway, and cry out, "No, no, no—not to-night; I cannot endure it yet!"

It was only when another and a fiercer jealousy was awakened in this woman's breast, that she arose all at once, strong, resolute, and undaunted, to do the work she had so miserably deferred. As one poison is said to neutralise the evil power of another, so Olivia Marchmont's jealousy of Belinda seemed to blot out and extinguish her hatred of Mary. Better anything than that Edward Arundel should have a new, and perhaps a fairer, bride. The jealous woman had always looked upon Mary Marchmont as a despicable rival. Better that Edward should be tied to this girl, than that he should rejoice in the smiles of a lovelier woman, worthier of his affection. *This* was the feeling paramount in Olivia's breast, although she was herself half unconscious how entirely this was the motive power which had given her new strength and resolution. She tried to think that it was the awakening of her conscience that had made her strong enough to do this one good work; but in the semi-darkness of her own mind there was still a feeble glimmer of the light of truth, and it was this that had prompted her to cry out on her knees before the altar in Hillingsworth church, and declare the sinfulness of her nature.

* * * * *

Paul Marchmont stopped several times before the ragged, untrimmed fruit-trees in his purposeless wanderings in the neglected garden at Stony Stringford, before the vaporous confusion cleared away from his brain, and he was able to understand what had happened to him.

His first reasonable action was to take out his watch; but even then he stood for some moments staring at the dial before he remembered why he had taken the watch from his pocket, or what it was that he wanted to know. By Mr.

Marchmont's chronometer it was ten minutes past seven o'clock; but the watch had been unwound upon the previous night, and had run down. Paul put it back in his waistcoat-pocket, and then walked slowly along the weedy pathway to that low latticed window in which he had often seen Mary Arundel standing with her child in her arms. He went to this window and looked in, with his face against the glass. The room was neat and orderly now; for the woman whom Mr. Marchmont had hired had gone about her work as usual, and was in the act of filling a little brown earthenware teapot from a kettle on the hob when Paul stared in at her.

She looked up as Mr. Marchmont's figure came between her and the light, and nearly dropped the little brown teapot in her terror of her offended employer.

But Paul pulled open the window, and spoke to her very quietly. "Stop where you are," he said; "I want to speak to you. I'll come in."

He went into the house by a door, that had once been the front and principal entrance, which opened into a low wainscoted hall. From this room he went into the parlour, which had been Mary Arundel's apartment, and in which the hired nurse was now preparing her breakfast. "I thought I might as well get a cup of tea, sir, whiles I waited for your orders," the woman murmured, apologetically; "for bein' knocked up so early this morning, you see, sir, has made my head *that* bad, I could scarcely bear myself; and——"

Paul lifted his hand to stop the woman's talk, as he had done before. He had no consciousness of what she was saying, but the sound of her voice pained him. His eyebrows contracted with a spasmodic action, as if something had hurt his head.

There was a Dutch clock in the corner of the room, with a long pendulum swinging against the wall. By this clock it was half-past eight.

"Is your clock right?" Paul asked.

"Yes, sir. Leastways, it may be five minutes too slow, but not more."

Mr. Marchmont took out his watch, wound it up, and regulated it by the Dutch clock.

"Now," he said, "perhaps you can tell me clearly what happened. I want no excuses, remember; I only want to know what occurred, and what was said— word for word, remember."

He sat down but got up again directly, and walked to the window; then he paced up and down the room two or three times, and then went back to the fireplace and sat down again. He was like a man who, in the racking torture of some physical pain, finds a miserable relief in his own restlessness.

"Come," he said; "I am waiting."

"Yes, sir; which, begging your parding, if you wouldn't mind sitting still like, while I'm a-telling of you, which it do remind me of the wild beastes in the Zoological, sir, to that degree, that the boil, to which I am subjeck, sir, and have been from a child, might prevent me bein' as truthful as I should wish. Mrs. Marchmont, sir, she come before it was light, *in* a cart, sir, which it was a shaycart, and made comfortable with cushions and straw, and suchlike, or I should not have let the young lady go away in it; and she bring with her a respectable, homely-looking young person, which she call Hester Jobling or Gobson, or somethink of that sound like, which my memory is treechrous, and I don't wish to tell a story on no account; and Mrs. Marchmont she go straight up to my young lady, and she shakes her by the shoulder; and then the young woman called Hester, she wakes up my young lady quite gentle like, and kisses her and cries over her; and a man as drove the cart, which looked a small tradesman well-to-do, brings his trap round to the front-door,—you may see the trax of the wheels upon the gravel now, sir, if you disbelieve me. And Mrs. Marchmont and the young woman called Hester, between 'em they gets my young lady up, and dresses her, and dresses the child; and does it all so quick, and overrides me to such a degree, that I hadn't no power to prevent 'em; but I say to Mrs. Marchmont, I say: 'Is it Mr. Marchmont's orders as his cousin should be took away this morning?' and she stare at me hard, and say, 'Yes;' and she have allus an abrumpt way, but was abrumpter than ordinary this morning. And, oh sir, bein' a poor lone woman, what was I to do?"

"Have you nothing more to tell me?"

"Nothing, sir; leastways, except as they lifted my young lady into the cart, and the man got in after 'em, and drove away as fast as his horse would go; and they had been gone two minutes when I began to feel all in a tremble like, for fear as I might have done wrong in lettin' of 'em go."

"You have done wrong," Paul answered, sternly; "but no matter. If these officious friends of my poor weak-witted cousin choose to take her away, so much the better for me, who have been burdened with her long enough. Since your charge has gone, your services are no longer wanted. I shan't act illiberally to you, though I am very much annoyed by your folly and stupidity. Is there anything due to you?"

Mrs. Brown hesitated for a moment, and then replied, in a very insinuating tone,—

"Not *wages*, sir; there ain't no *wages* doo to me,—which you paid me a quarter in advance last Saturday was a week, and took a receipt, sir, for the amount. But I have done my dooty, sir, and had but little sleep and rest, which my 'ealth ain't what it was when I answered your advertisement, requirin' a respectable motherly person, to take charge of a invalid lady, not objectin' to the country—which I freely tell you, sir, if I'd known that the country was a rheumatic old place like this, with rats enough to scare away a regyment of soldiers, I would not have undertook the situation; so any present as you might think sootable, considerin' all things, and——"

"That will do," said Paul Marchmont, taking a handful of loose money from his waistcoat pocket; "I suppose a ten-pound note would satisfyyou?"

"Indeed it would, sir, and very liberal of you too——"

"Very well. I've got a five-pound note here, and five sovereigns. The best thing you can do is to get back to London at once; there's a train leaves Milsome Station at eleven o'clock—Milsome's not more than a mile and a half from here. You can get your things together; there's a boy about the place who will carry them for you, I suppose?"

"Yes, sir; there's a boy by the name of William."

"He can go with you, then; and if you look sharp, you can catch the eleven-o'clock train."

"Yes, sir; and thank you kindly, sir."

"I don't want any thanks. See that you don't miss the train; that's all you have to take care of."

Mr. Marchmont went out into the garden again. He had done something, at any rate; he had arranged for getting this woman out of the way.

If—if by any remote chance there might be yet a possibility of keeping the secret of Mary's existence, here was one witness already got rid of.

But was there any chance? Mr. Marchmont sat down on a rickety old garden-seat, and tried to think—tried to take a deliberate survey of his position.

No; there was no hope for him. Look which way he could, there was not one ray of light. With George Weston and Olivia, Betsy Murrel the servant-girl, and Hester Jobson to bear witness against him, what could he hope?

The surgeon would be able to declare that the child was Mary's son, her legitimate son, sole heir to that estate of which Paul had taken possession.

There was no hope. There was no possibility that Olivia should waver in her purpose; for had she not brought with her two witnesses—Hester Jobson and her husband?

From that moment the case was taken out of her hands. The honest carpenter and his wife would see that Mary had her rights.

"It will be a glorious speculation for them," thought Paul Marchmont, who naturally measured other people's characters by a standard derived from an accurate knowledge of his own.

Yes, his ruin was complete. Destruction had come upon him, swift and sudden as the caprice of a madwoman—or—the thunderbolt of an offended Providence. What should he do? Run away, sneak away by back-lanes and narrow footpaths to the nearest railway-station, hide himself in a third-class carriage going Londonwards, and from London get away to Liverpool, to creep on board some emigrant vessel bound for New York?

He could not even do this, for he was without the means of getting so much as the railway-ticket that should carry him on the first stage of his flight. After having given ten pounds to Mrs. Brown, he had only a few shillings in his waistcoat-pocket. He had only one article of any great value about him, and that was his watch, which had cost fifty pounds. But the Marchmont arms were emblazoned on the outside of the case; and Paul's name in full, and the address of Marchmont Towers, were ostentatiously engraved inside, so that any attempt to dispose of the watch must inevitably lead to the identification of the owner.

Paul Marchmont had made no provision for this evil day. Supreme in the consciousness of his own talents, he had never imagined discovery and destruction. His plans had been so well arranged. On the very day after Edward's second marriage, Mary and her child would have been conveyed away to the remotest district in Wales; and the artist would have laughed at the idea of danger. The shallowest schemer might have been able to manage this poor broken-hearted girl, whose many sorrows had brought her to look upon life as a thing which was never meant to be joyful, and which was only to be endured patiently, like some slow disease that would be surely cured in the grave. It had been so easy to deal with this ignorant and gentle victim that Paul had grown bold and confident, and had ignored the possibility of such ruin as had now come down upon him.

What was he to do? What was the nature of his crime, and what penalty had he incurred? He tried to answer these questions; but as his offence was of no common kind, he knew of no common law which could apply to it. Was it a felony, this appropriation of another person's property, this concealment of another person's existence; or was it only a conspiracy, amenable to no criminal law; and would he be called upon merely to make restitution of that which he had spent and wasted? What did it matter? Either way, there was nothing for him but ruin—irretrievable ruin.

There are some men who can survive discovery and defeat, and begin a new life in a new world, and succeed in a new career. But Paul Marchmont was not one of these. He could not stick a hunting-knife and a brace of revolvers in his leathern belt, sling a game-bag across his shoulders, take up his breech-loading rifle, and go out into the backwoods of an uncivilised country, to turn sheep-breeder, and hold his own against a race of agricultural savages. He was a Cockney, and for him there was only one world—a world in which men wore varnished boots and enamelled shirt-studs with portraits of La Montespan or La Dubarry, and lived in chambers in the Albany, and treated each other to little dinners at Greenwich and Richmond, or cut a grand figure at a country-house, and collected a gallery of art and a museum of *bric à brac*. This was the world upon the outer edge of which Paul Marchmont had lived so long, looking in at the brilliant inhabitants with hungry, yearning eyes through all the days of his poverty and obscurity. This was the world into which he had pushed himself at last by means of a crime.

He was forty years of age; and in all his life he had never had but one ambition,—and that was to be master of Marchmont Towers. The remote chance of that inheritance had hung before him ever since his boyhood, a glittering prize, far away in the distance, but so brilliant as to blind him to the brightness of all nearer chances. Why should he slave at his easel, and toil to become a great painter? When would art earn him eleven thousand a year? The greatest painter of Mr. Marchmont's time lived in a miserable lodging at Chelsea. It was before the days of the "Railway Station" and the "Derby Day;" or perhaps Paul might have made an effort to become that which Heaven never meant him to be—a great painter. No; art was only a means of living with this man. He painted, and sold his pictures to his few patrons, who beat him down unmercifully, giving him a small profit upon his canvas and colours, for the encouragement of native art; but he only painted to live.

He was waiting. From the time when he could scarcely speak plain, Marchmont Towers had been a familiar word in his ears and on his lips. He knew the number of lives that stood between his father and the estate, and had learned to say, naïvely enough then,—

"O pa, don't you wish that Uncle Philip and Uncle Marmaduke and Cousin John would die soon?"

He was two-and-twenty years of age when his father died; and he felt a faint thrill of satisfaction, even in the midst of his sorrow, at the thought that there was one life the less between him and the end of his hopes. But other lives had sprung up in the interim. There was young Arthur, and little Mary; and Marchmont Towers was like a caravanserai in the desert, which seems to be farther and farther away as the weary traveller strives to reach it.

Still Paul hoped, and watched, and waited. He had all the instincts of a sybarite, and he fancied, therefore, that he was destined to be a rich man. He

113

watched, and waited, and hoped, and cheered his mother and sister when they were downcast with the hope of better days. When the chance came, he seized upon it, and plotted, and succeeded, and revelled in his brief success.

But now ruin had come to him, what was he to do? He tried to make some plan for his own conduct; but he could not. His brain reeled with the effort which he made to realise his own position.

He walked up and down one of the pathways in the garden until a quarter to ten o'clock; then he went into the house, and waited till Mrs. Brown had departed from Stony-Stringford Farm, attended by the boy, who carried two bundles, a bandbox, and a carpet-bag.

"Come back here when you have taken those things to the station," Paul said; "I shall want you."

He watched the dilapidated five-barred gate swing to after the departure of Mrs. Brown and her attendant, and then went to look at his horse. The patient animal had been standing in a shed all this time, and had had neither food nor water. Paul searched amongst the empty barns and outhouses, and found a few handfuls of fodder. He took this to the animal, and then went back again to the garden,—to that quiet garden, where the bees were buzzing about in the sunshine with a drowsy, booming sound, and where a great tabby-cat was sleeping stretched flat upon its side, on one of the flower-beds.

Paul Marchmont waited here very impatiently till the boy came back.

"I must see Lavinia," he thought. "I dare not leave this place till I have seen Lavinia. I don't know what may be happening at Hillingsworth or Kemberling. These things are taken up sometimes by the populace. They may make a party against me; they may—"

He stood still, gnawing the edges of his nails, and staring down at the gravel-walk.

He was thinking of things that he had read in the newspapers,—cases in which some cruel mother who had illused her child, or some suspected assassin who, in all human probability, had poisoned his wife, had been well-nigh torn piecemeal by an infuriated mob, and had been glad to cling for protection to the officers of justice, or to beg leave to stay in prison after acquittal, for safe shelter from honest men and women's indignation.

He remembered one special case in which the populace, unable to get at a man's person, tore down his house, and vented their fury upon unsentient bricks and mortar.

Mr. Marchmont took out a little memorandum book, and scrawled a few lines in pencil:

"I am here, at Stony-Stringford Farmhouse," he wrote. "For God's sake, come to me, Lavinia, and at once; you can drive here yourself. I want to know what has happened at Kemberling and at Hillingsworth. Find out everything for me, and come. P. M."

It was nearly twelve o'clock when the boy returned. Paul gave him this letter, and told the lad to get on his own horse, and ride to Kemberling as fast as he could go. He was to leave the horse at Kemberling, in Mr. Weston's stable, and was to come back to Stony-Stringford with Mrs. Weston. This order Paul particularly impressed upon the boy, lest he should stop in Kemberling, and reveal the secret of Paul's hiding-place.

Mr. Paul Marchmont was afraid. A terrible sickening dread had taken possession of him, and what little manliness there had ever been in his nature seemed to have deserted him to-day.

Oh, the long dreary hours of that miserable day! the hideous sunshine, that scorched Mr. Marchmont's bare head, as he loitered about the garden!—he had left his hat in the house; but he did not even know that he was bareheaded. Oh, the misery of that long day of suspense and anguish! The sick consciousness of utter defeat, the thought of the things that he might have done, the purse that he might have made with the money that he had lavished on pictures, and decorations, and improvements, and the profligate extravagance of splendid entertainments. This is what he thought of, and these were the thoughts that tortured him. But in all that miserable day he never felt one pang of remorse for the agonies that he had inflicted upon his innocent victim; on the contrary, he hated her because of this discovery, and gnashed his teeth as he thought how she and her young husband would enjoy all the grandeur of Marchmont Towers,—all that noble revenue which he had hoped to hold till his dying day.

It was growing dusk when Mr. Marchmont heard the sound of wheels in the dusty lane outside the garden-wall. He went through the house, and into the farmyard, in time to receive his sister Lavinia at the gate. It was the wheels of her pony-carriage he had heard. She drove a pair of ponies, which Paul had given her. He was angry with himself as he remembered that this was another piece of extravagance,—another sum of money recklessly squandered, when it might have gone towards the making of a rich provision for this evil day.

Mrs. Weston was very pale; and her brother could see by her face that she brought him no good news. She left her ponies to the care of the boy, and went into the garden with her brother.

"Well, Lavinia?"

"Well, Paul, it is a dreadful business," Mrs. Weston said, in a low voice.

"It's all George's doing! It's all the work of that infernal scoundrel!" cried Paul, passionately. "But he shall pay bitterly for——"

"Don't let us talk of him, Paul; no good can come of that. What are you going to do?"

"I don't know. I sent for you because I wanted your help and advice. What's the good of your coming if you bring me no help?"

"Don't be cruel, Paul. Heaven knows, I'll do my best. But I can't see what's to be done—except for you to get away, Paul. Everything's known. Olivia stopped the marriage publicly in Hillingsworth Church; and all the Hillingsworth people followed Edward Arundel's carriage to Kemberling. The report spread like wildfire; and, oh Paul, the Kemberling people have taken it up, and our windows have been broken, and there's been a crowd all day upon the terrace before the Towers, and they've tried to get into the house, declaring that they know you're hiding somewhere. Paul, Paul, what are we to do? The people hooted after me as I drove away from the High Street, and the boys threw stones at the ponies. Almost all the servants have left the Towers. The constables have been up there trying to get the crowd off the terrace. But what are we to do, Paul? what are we to do?"

"Kill ourselves," answered the artist savagely. "What else should we do? What have we to live for? You have a little money, I suppose; I have none. Do you think I can go back to the old life? Do you think I can go back, and live in that shabby house in Charlotte Street, and paint the same rocks and boulders, the same long stretch of sea, the same low lurid streaks of light,—all the old subjects over again,—for the same starvation prices? Do you think I can ever tolerate shabby clothes again, or miserable make-shift dinners,—hashed mutton, with ill-cut hunks of lukewarm meat floating about in greasy slop called gravy, and washed down with flat porter fetched half an hour too soon from a public-house,—do you think I can go back to *that*? No; I have tasted the wine of life: I have lived; and I'll never go back to the living death called poverty. Do you think I can stand in that passage in Charlotte Street again, Lavinia, to be bullied by an illiterate tax-gatherer, or insulted by an infuriated baker? No, Lavinia; I have made my venture, and I have failed."

"But what will you do, Paul?"

"I don't know," he answered, moodily.

This was a lie. He knew well enough what he meant to do: he would kill himself.

That resolution inspired him with a desperate kind of courage. He would escape from the mob; he would get away somewhere or other quietly and there kill himself. He didn't know how, as yet; but he would deliberate upon that point at his leisure, and choose the death that was supposed to be least painful.

"Where are my mother and Clarissa?" he asked presently.

"They are at our house; they came to me directly they heard the rumour of what had happened. I don't know how they heard it; but every one heard of it, simultaneously, as it seemed. My mother is in a dreadful state. I dared not tell her that I had known it all along."

"Oh, of course not," answered Paul, with a sneer; "let me bear the burden of my guilt alone. What did my mother say?"

"She kept saying again and again, 'I can't believe it. I can't believe that he could do anything cruel; he has been such a good son.'"

"I was not cruel," Paul cried vehemently; "the girl had every comfort. I never grudged money for her comfort. She was a miserable, apathetic creature, to whom fortune was almost a burden rather than an advantage. If I separated her from her husband—bah!—was that such a cruelty? She was no worse off than if Edward Arundel had been killed in that railway accident; and it might have been so."

He didn't waste much time by reasoning on this point. He thought of his mother and sisters. From first to last he had been a good son and a good brother.

"What money have you, Lavinia?"

"A good deal; you have been very generous to me, Paul; and you shall have it all back again, if you want it. I have got upwards of two thousand pounds altogether; for I have been very careful of the money you have given me."

"You have been wise. Now listen to me, Lavinia. I *have* been a good son, and I have borne my burdens uncomplainingly. It is your turn now to bear yours. I must get back to Marchmont Towers, if I can, and gather together whatever personal property I have there. It isn't much—only a few trinkets, and suchlike. You must send me some one you can trust to fetch those to-night; for I shall not stay an hour in the place. I may not even be admitted into it; for Edward Arundel may have already taken possession in his wife's name. Then you will have to decide where you are to go. You can't stay in this part of the country. Weston must be liable to some penalty or other for his share in the business, unless he's bought over as a witness to testify to the identity of Mary's child. I haven't time to think of all this. I want you to promise me that you will take care of your mother and your invalid sister."

"I will, Paul; I will indeed. But tell me what you are going to do yourself, and where you are going?"

"I don't know," Paul Marchmont answered, in the same tone as before; "but whatever I do, I want you to give me your solemn promise that you will be good to my mother and sister."

"I will, Paul; I promise you to do as you have done."

"You had better leave Kemberling by the first train to-morrow morning; take my mother and Clarissa with you; take everything that is worth taking, and leave Weston behind you to bear the brunt of this business. You can get a lodging in the old neighbourhood, and no one will molest you when you once get away from this place. But remember one thing, Lavinia: if Mary Arundel's child should die, and Mary herself should die childless, Clarissa will inherit Marchmont Towers. Don't forget that. There's a chance yet for you: it's far away, and unlikely enough; but it *is* a chance."

"But you are more likely to outlive Mary and her child than Clarissa is," Mrs. Weston answered, with a feeble attempt at hopefulness; "try and think of that, Paul, and let the hope cheer you."

"Hope!" cried Mr. Marchmont, with a discordant laugh. "Yes; I'm forty years old, and for five-and-thirty of those years I've hoped and waited for Marchmont Towers. I can't hope any longer, or wait any longer. I give it up; I've fought hard, but I'm beaten."

It was nearly dark by this time, the shadowy darkness of a midsummer's evening; and there were stars shining faintly out of the sky.

"You can drive me back to the Towers," Paul Marchmont said. "I don't want to lose any time in getting there; I may be locked out by Mr. Edward Arundel if I don't take care."

Mrs. Weston and her brother went back to the farmyard. It was sixteen miles from Kemberling to Stony Stringford; and the ponies were steaming, for Lavinia had come at a good rate. But it was no time for the consideration of horseflesh. Paul took a rug from the empty seat, and wrapped himself in it. He would not be likely to be recognised in the darkness, sitting back in the low seat, and made bulky by the ponderous covering in which he had enveloped himself. Mrs. Weston took the whip from the boy, gathered up the reins, and drove off. Paul had left no orders about the custody of the old farmhouse. The boy went home to his master, at the other end of the farm; and the night-winds wandered wherever they listed through the deserted habitation.

CHAPTER XIV.

THERE IS CONFUSION WORSE THAN DEATH.

The brother and sister exchanged very few words during the drive between Stony Stringford and Marchmont Towers. It was arranged between them that Mrs. Weston should drive by a back-way leading to a lane that skirted the edge of the river, and that Paul should get out at a gate opening into the wood, and by that means make his way, unobserved, to the house which had so lately been to all intents and purposes his own.

He dared not attempt to enter the Towers by any other way; for the indignant populace might still be lurking about the front of the house, eager to inflict summary vengeance upon the persecutor of a helpless girl.

It was between nine and ten o'clock when Mr. Marchmont got out at the little gate. All here was very still; and Paul heard the croaking of the frogs upon the margin of a little pool in the wood, and the sound of horses' hoofs a mile away upon the loose gravel by the water-side.

"Good night, Lavinia," he said. "Send for the things as soon as you go back; and be sure you send a safe person for them."

"O yes, dear; but hadn't you better take any thing of value yourself?" Mrs. Weston asked anxiously. "You say you have no money. Perhaps it would be best for you to send me the jewellery, though, and I can send you what money you want by my messenger."

"I shan't want any money—at least I have enough for what I want. What have you done with your savings?"

"They are in a London bank. But I have plenty of ready money in the house. You must want money, Paul?"

"I tell you, no; I have as much as I want."

"But tell me your plans, Paul; I must know your plans before I leave Lincolnshire myself. Are *you* going away?"

"Yes."

"Immediately?"

"Immediately."

"Shall you go to London?"

"Perhaps. I don't know yet."

"But when shall we see you again, Paul? or how shall we hear of you?"

"I'll write to you."

"Where?"

"At the Post-office in Rathbone Place. Don't bother me with a lot of questions to-night Lavinia; I'm not in the humour to answer them."

Paul Marchmont turned away from his sister impatiently, and opened the gate; but before she had driven off, he went back to her.

"Shake hands, Lavinia," he said; "shake hands, my dear; it may be a long time before you and I meet again."

He bent down and kissed his sister.

"Drive home as fast as you can, and send the messenger directly. He had better come to the door of the lobby, near Olivia's room. Where is Olivia, by-the-bye? Is she still with the stepdaughter she loves so dearly?"

"No; she went to Swampington early in the afternoon. A fly was ordered from the Black Bull, and she went away in it."

"So much the better," answered Mr. Marchmont. "Good night, Lavinia. Don't let my mother think ill of me. I tried to do the best I could to make her happy. Good-bye."

"Good-bye, dear Paul; God bless you!"

The blessing was invoked with as much sincerity as if Lavinia Weston had been a good woman, and her brother a good man. Perhaps neither of those two was able to realise the extent of the crime which they had assisted each other to commit.

Mrs. Weston drove away; and Paul went up to the back of the Towers, and under an archway leading into the quadrangle. All about the house was as quiet as if the Sleeping Beauty and her court had been its only occupants.

The inhabitants of Kemberling and the neighbourhood were an orderly people, who burnt few candles between May and September; and however much they might have desired to avenge Mary Arundel's wrongs by tearing Paul Marchmont to pieces, their patience had been exhausted by nightfall, and they had been glad to return to their respective abodes, to discuss Paul's iniquities comfortably over the nine-o'clock beer.

Paul stood still in the quadrangle for a few moments, and listened. He could hear no human breath or whisper; he only heard the sound of the corn-crake in the fields to the right of the Towers, and the distant rumbling of wagon-wheels on the high-road. There was a glimmer of light in one of the windows belonging to the servants' offices,—only one dim glimmer, where there had usually been a row of brilliantly-lighted casements. Lavinia was right, then; almost all the servants had left the Towers. Paul tried to open the half-glass door leading into the lobby; but it was locked. He rang a bell; and after about three minutes' delay, a buxom country-girl appeared in the lobby carrying a candle. She was some kitchenmaid or dairymaid or scullerymaid, whom Paul could not remember to have ever seen until now. She opened the door, and admitted him, dropping a curtsey as he passed her. There was some relief even in this. Mr. Marchmont had scarcely expected to get into the house at all; still less to be received with common civility by any of the servants, who had so lately obeyed him and fawned upon him.

"Where are all the rest of the servants?" he asked.

"They're all gone, sir; except him as you brought down from London,—Mr. Peterson,—and me and mother. Mother's in the laundry, sir; and I'm scullerymaid."

"Why did the other servants leave the place?"

"Mostly because they was afraid of the mob upon the terrace, I think, sir; for there's been people all the afternoon throwin' stones, and breakin' the windows; and I don't think as there's a whole pane of glass in the front of the house, sir; and Mr. Gormby, sir, he come about four o'clock, and he got the people to go away, sir, by tellin' 'em as it wern't your property, sir, but the young lady's, Miss Mary Marchmont,—leastways, Mrs. Airendale,—as they was destroyin' of; but most of the servants had gone before that, sir, except Mr. Peterson; and Mr. Gormby gave orders as me and mother was to lock all the doors, and let no one in upon no account whatever; and he's coming to-morrow mornin' to take possession, he says; and please, sir, you can't come in; for his special orders to me and mother was, no one, and you in particklar."

"Nonsense, girl!" exclaimed Mr. Marchmont, decisively; "who is Mr. Gormby, that he should give orders as to who comes in or stops out? I'm only coming in for half an hour, to pack my portmanteau. Where's Peterson?"

"In the dinin'-room, sir; but please, sir, you mustn't——"

The girl made a feeble effort to intercept Mr. Marchmont, in accordance with the steward's special orders; which were, that Paul should, upon no pretence whatever, be suffered to enter the house. But the artist snatched the candlestick from her hand, and went towards the dining-room, leaving her to stare after him in amazement.

Paul found his valet Peterson, taking what he called a snack, in the dining-room. A cloth was spread upon the corner of the table; and there was a fore-quarter of cold roast-lamb, a bottle of French brandy, and a decanter half-full of Madeira before the valet.

He started as his master entered the room, and looked up, not very respectfully, but with no unfriendly glance.

"Give me half a tumbler of that brandy, Peterson," said Mr. Marchmont.

The man obeyed; and Paul drained the fiery spirit as if it had been so much water. It was four-and-twenty hours since meat or drink had crossed his dry white lips.

"Why didn't you go away with the rest?" he asked, as he set down the empty glass.

"It's only rats, sir, that run away from a falling house. I stopped, thinkin' you'd be goin' away somewhere, and that you'd want me."

The solid and unvarnished truth of the matter was, that Peterson had taken it for granted that his master had made an excellent purse against this evil day, and would be ready to start for the Continent or America, there to lead a pleasant life upon the proceeds of his iniquity. The valet never imagined his master guilty of such besotted folly as to be _un_prepared for this catastrophe.

"I thought you might still want me, sir," he said; "and wherever you're going, I'm quite ready to go too. You've been a good master to me, sir; and I don't want to leave a good master because things go against him."

Paul Marchmont shook his head, and held out the empty tumbler for his servant to pour more brandy into it.

"I am going away," he said; "but I want no servant where I'm going; but I'm grateful to you for your offer, Peterson. Will you come upstairs with me? I want to pack a few things."

"They're all packed, sir. I knew you'd be leaving, and I've packed everything."

"My dressing-case?"

"Yes, sir. You've got the key of that."

"Yes; I know, I know."

Paul Marchmont was silent for a few minutes, thinking. Everything that he had in the way of personal property of any value was in the dressing-case of which he had spoken. There was five or six hundred pounds' worth of jewellery in Mr. Marchmont's dressing-case; for the first instinct of the *nouveau riche* exhibits itself in diamond shirt-studs, cameo rings, malachite death's-heads with emerald eyes; grotesque and pleasing charms in the form of coffins, coal-scuttles, and hobnailed boots; fantastical lockets of ruby and enamel; wonderful bands of massive yellow gold, studded with diamonds, wherein to insert the two ends of flimsy lace cravats. Mr. Marchmont reflected upon the amount of his possessions, and their security in the jewel-drawer of his dressing-case. The dressing-case was furnished with a Chubb's lock, the key of which he carried in his waistcoat-pocket. Yes, it was all safe.

"Look here, Peterson," said Paul Marchmont; "I think I shall sleep at Mrs. Weston's to-night. I should like you to take my dressing-case down there at once."

"And how about the other luggage, sir,—the portmanteaus and hat-boxes?"

"Never mind those. I want you to put the dressing-case safe in my sister's hands. I can send here for the rest to-morrow morning. You needn't wait for me now. I'll follow you in half an hour."

"Yes, sir. You want the dressing-case carried to Mrs. Weston's house, and I'm to wait for you there?"

"Yes; you can wait for me."

"But is there nothing else I can do, sir?"

"Nothing whatever. I've only got to collect a few papers, and then I shall follow you."

"Yes, sir."

The discreet Peterson bowed, and retired to fetch the dressing-case. He put his own construction upon Mr. Marchmont's evident desire to get rid of him, and to be left alone at the Towers. Paul had, of course, made a purse, and had doubtless put his money away in some very artful hiding-place, whence he now wanted to take it at his leisure. He had stuffed one of his pillows with bank-notes, perhaps; or had hidden a cash-box behind the tapestry in his bedchamber; or had buried a bag of gold in the flower-garden below the terrace. Mr. Peterson went upstairs to Paul's dressing-room, put his hand through the strap of the dressing-case, which was very heavy, went downstairs again, met his master in the hall, and went out at the lobby-door.

Paul locked the door upon his valet, and then went back into the lonely house, where the ticking of the clocks in the tenantless rooms sounded unnaturally loud in the stillness. All the windows had been broken; and though the shutters were shut, the cold night-air blew in at many a crack and cranny, and well-nigh extinguished Mr. Marchmont's candle as he went from room to room looking about him.

He went into the western drawing-room, and lighted some of the lamps in the principal chandelier. The shutters were shut, for the windows here, as well as elsewhere, had been broken; fragments of shivered glass, great jagged stones, and handfuls of gravel, lay about upon the rich carpet,—the velvet-pile which he had chosen with such artistic taste, such careful deliberation. He lit the lamps and walked about the room, looking for the last time at his treasures. Yes, *his* treasures. It was he who had transformed this chamber from a prim, old-fashioned sitting-room—with quaint japanned cabinets, shabby chintz-cushioned cane-chairs, cracked Indian vases, and a faded carpet—into a saloon that would have been no discredit to Buckingham Palace or Alton Towers.

It was he who had made the place what it was. He had squandered the savings of Mary's minority upon pictures that the richest collector in England might have been proud to own; upon porcelain that would have been worthy of a place in the Vienna Museum or the Bernal Collection. He had done this, and these things were to pass into the possession of the man he hated,—the fiery young soldier who had horsewhipped him before the face of wondering Lincolnshire. He walked about the room, thinking of his life since he had come into possession of this place, and of what it had been before that time, and what it must be again, unless he summoned up a desperate courage—and killed himself.

His heart beat fast and loud, and he felt an icy chill creeping slowly through his every vein as he thought of this. How was he to kill himself? He had no poison in his possession,—no deadly drug that would reduce the agony of death to the space of a lightning-flash. There were pistols, rare gems of choicest workmanship, in one of the buhl-cabinets in that very room; there were both fowling-piece and ammunition in Mr. Marchmont's dressing-room: but the artist was not expert with the use of firearms, and he might fail in the attempt to blow out his brains, and only maim or disfigure himself hideously. There was the river,—the black, sluggish river: but then, drowning is a slow death, and Heaven only knows how long the agony may seem to the wretch who endures it! Alas! the ghastly truth of the matter is that Mr. Marchmont was afraid of death. Look at the King of Terrors how he would, he could not discover any pleasing aspect under which he could meet the grim monarch without flinching.

He looked at life; but if life was less terrible than death, it was not less dreary. He looked forward with a shudder to see—what? Humiliation, disgrace, perhaps punishment,—life-long transportation, it may be; for this base conspiracy might be a criminal offence, amenable to criminal law. Or, escaping all this, what was there for him? What was there for this man even then? For forty years he had been steeped to the lips in poverty, and had endured his life. He looked back now, and wondered how it was that he had been patient; he wondered why he had not made an end of himself and his obscure troubles twenty years before this night. But after looking back a little longer, he saw the star which had illumined the darkness of that miserable and sordid existence, and he understood the reason of his endurance. He had hoped. Day after day he had got up to go through the same troubles, to endure the same humiliations: but every day, when his life had been hardest to him, he had said, "To-morrow I may be master of Marchmont Towers." But he could never hope this any more; he could not go back to watch and wait again, beguiled by the faint hope that Mary Arundel's son might die, and to hear by-and-by that other children were born to her to widen the great gulf betwixt him and fortune.

He looked back, and he saw that he had lived from day to day, from year to year, lured on by this one hope. He looked forward, and he saw that he could not live without it.

There had never been but this one road to good fortune open to him. He was a clever man, but his was not the cleverness which can transmute itself into solid cash. He could only paint indifferent pictures; and he had existed long enough by picture-painting to realise the utter hopelessness of success in that career.

He had borne his life while he was in it, but he could not bear to go back to it. He had been out of it, and had tasted another phase of existence; and he could see it all now plainly, as if he had been a spectator sitting in the boxes and watching a dreary play performed upon a stage before him. The performers in the remotest provincial theatre believe in the play they are acting. The omnipotence of passion creates dewy groves and moonlit atmospheres, ducal robes and beautiful women. But the metropolitan spectator, in whose mind the memory of better things is still fresh, sees that the moonlit trees are poor distemper daubs, pushed on by dirty carpenters, and the moon a green bottle borrowed from a druggist's shop, the ducal robes threadbare cotton velvet and tarnished tinsel, and the heroine of the drama old and ugly.

So Paul looked at the life he had endured, and wondered as he saw how horrible it was.

He could see the shabby lodging, the faded furniture, the miserable handful of fire struggling with the smoke in a shallow grate, that had been half-blocked up with bricks by some former tenant as badly off as himself. He could look back at that dismal room, with the ugly paper on the walls, the scanty curtains flapping in the wind which they pretended to shut out; the figure of his mother sitting near the fireplace, with that pale, anxious face, which was a perpetual complaint against hardship and discomfort. He could see his sister standing at the window in the dusky twilight, patching up some worn-out garment, and straining her eyes for the sake of economising in the matter of half an inch of candle. And the street below the window,—the shabby-genteel street, with a dingy shop breaking out here and there, and children playing on the doorsteps, and a muffin-bell jingling through the evening fog, and a melancholy Italian grinding "Home, sweet Home!" in the patch of lighted road opposite the pawnbroker's. He saw it all; and it was all alike—sordid, miserable, hopeless.

Paul Marchmont had never sunk so low as his cousin John. He had never descended so far in the social scale as to carry a banner at Drury Lane, or to live in one room in Oakley Street, Lambeth. But there had been times when to pay the rent of three rooms had been next kin to an impossibility to the artist, and when the honorarium of a shilling a night would have been very acceptable to him. He had drained the cup of poverty to the dregs; and now the cup was filled again, and the bitter draught was pushed once more into his unwilling hand.

He must drink that, or another potion,—a sleeping-draught, which is commonly called Death. He must die! But how? His coward heart sank as the awful alternative pressed closer upon him. He must die!—to-night,—at once, —in that house; so that when they came in the morning to eject him, they would have little trouble; they would only have to carry out a corpse.

He walked up and down the room, biting his finger-nails to the quick, but coming to no resolution, until he was interrupted by the ringing of the bell at the lobby-door. It was the messenger from his sister, no doubt. Paul drew his watch from his waistcoat-pocket, unfastened his chain, took a set of gold-studs from the breast of his shirt, and a signet-ring from his finger; then he sat down at a writing-table, and packed the watch and chain, the studs and signet-ring, and a bunch of keys, in a large envelope. He sealed this packet, and addressed it to his sister; then he took a candle, and went to the lobby. Mrs. Weston had sent a young man who was an assistant and pupil of her husband's—a good-tempered young fellow, who willingly served her in her hour of trouble. Paul gave this messenger the key of his dressing-case and packet.

"You will be sure and put that in my sister's hands," he said.

"O yes, sir. Mrs. Weston gave me this letter for you, sir. Am I to wait for an answer?"

"No; there will be no answer. Good night."

"Good night, sir."

The young man went away; and Paul Marchmont heard him whistle a popular melody as he walked along the cloistered way and out of the quadrangle by a low archway commonly used by the tradespeople who came to the Towers.

The artist stood and listened to the young man's departing footsteps. Then, with a horrible thrill of anguish, he remembered that he had seen his last of humankind—he had heard his last of human voices: for he was to kill himself that night. He stood in the dark lobby, looking out into the quadrangle. He was quite alone in the house; for the girl who had let him in was in the laundry with her mother. He could see the figures of the two women moving about in a great gaslit chamber upon the other side of the quadrangle—a building which had no communication with the rest of the house. He was to die that night; and he had not yet even determined how he was to die.

He mechanically opened Mrs. Weston's letter: it was only a few lines, telling him that Peterson had arrived with the portmanteau and dressing-case, and that there would be a comfortable room prepared for him. "I am so glad you have changed your mind, and are coming to me, Paul," Mrs. Weston concluded. "Your manner, when we parted to-night, almost alarmed me."

Paul groaned aloud as he crushed the letter in his hand. Then he went back to the western drawing-room. He heard strange noises in the empty rooms as he passed by their open doors, weird creaking sounds and melancholy moanings in the wide chimneys. It seemed as if all the ghosts of Marchmont Towers were astir to-night, moved by an awful prescience of some coming horror.

Paul Marchmont was an atheist; but atheism, although a very pleasant theme for a critical and argumentative discussion after a lobster-supper and unlimited champagne, is but a poor staff to lean upon when the worn-out traveller approaches the mysterious portals of the unknown land.

The artist had boasted of his belief in annihilation; and had declared himself perfectly satisfied with a materialistic or pantheistic arrangement of the universe, and very indifferent as to whether he cropped up in future years as a summer-cabbage, or a new Raphael; so long as the ten stone or so of matter of which he was composed was made use of somehow or other, and did its duty in the great scheme of a scientific universe. But, oh! how that empty, soulless creed slipped away from him now, when he stood alone in this tenantless house, shuddering at strange spirit-noises, and horrified by a host of mystic fears—gigantic, shapeless terrors—that crowded in his empty, godless mind, and filled it with their hideous presence!

He had refused to believe in a personal God. He had laughed at the idea that there was any Deity to whom the individual can appeal, in his hour of grief or trouble, with the hope of any separate mercy, any special grace. He had rejected the Christian's simple creed, and now—now that he had floated away from the shores of life, and felt himself borne upon an irresistible current to that mysterious other side, what did he *not* believe in?

Every superstition that has ever disturbed the soul of ignorant man lent some one awful feature to the crowd of hideous images uprising in this man's mind: —awful Chaldean gods and Carthaginian goddesses, thirsting for the hot blood of human sacrifices, greedy for hecatombs of children flung shrieking into fiery furnaces, or torn limb from limb by savage beasts; Babylonian abominations; Egyptian Isis and Osiris; classical divinities, with flaming swords and pale impassible faces, rigid as the Destiny whose type they were; ghastly Germanic demons and witches.—All the dread avengers that man, in the knowledge of his own wickedness, has ever shadowed for himself out of the darkness of his ignorant mind, swelled that ghastly crowd, until the artist's brain reeled, and he was fain to sit with his head in his hands, trying, by a great effort of the will, to exorcise these loathsome phantoms.

"I must be going mad," he muttered to himself. "I am going mad."

But still the great question was unanswered—How was he to kill himself?

"I must settle that," he thought. "I dare not think of anything that may come afterwards. Besides, what *should* come? I *know* that there is nothing. Haven't I heard it demonstrated by cleverer men than I am? Haven't I looked at it in every light, and weighed it in every scale—always with the same result? Yes; I know that there is nothing *after* the one short pang, any more than there is pain in the nerve of a tooth when the tooth is gone. The nerve was the soul of the tooth, I suppose; but wrench away the body, and the soul is dead. Why should I be afraid? One short pain—it will seem long, I dare say—and then I shall lie still for ever and ever, and melt slowly back into the elements out of which I was created. Yes; I shall lie still—and be *nothing*."

Paul Marchmont sat thinking of this for a long time. Was it such a great advantage, after all, this annihilation, the sovereign good of the atheist's barren creed? It seemed to-night to this man as if it would be better to be anything—to suffer any anguish, any penalty for his sins, than to be blotted out for ever and ever from any conscious part in the grand harmony of the universe. If he could have believed in that Roman Catholic doctrine of purgatory, and that after cycles of years of suffering he might rise at last, purified from his sins, worthy to dwell among the angels, how differently would death have appeared to him! He might have gone away to hide himself in some foreign city, to perform patient daily sacrifices, humble acts of self-abnegation, every one of which should be a new figure, however small a one, to be set against the great sum of his sin.

But he could not believe. There is a vulgar proverb which says, "You cannot have your loaf and eat it;" or if proverbs would only be grammatical, it might be better worded, "You cannot eat your loaf, and have it to eat on some future occasion." Neither can you indulge in rationalistic discussions or epigrammatic pleasantry about the Great Creator who made you, and then turn and cry aloud to Him in the dreadful hour of your despair: "O my God, whom I have insulted and offended, help the miserable wretch who for twenty years has obstinately shut his heart against Thee!" It may be that God would forgive and hear even at that last supreme moment, as He heard the penitent thief upon the cross; but the penitent thief had been a sinner, not an unbeliever, and he *could* pray. The hard heart of the atheist freezes in his breast when he would repent and put away his iniquities. When he would fain turn to his offended Maker, the words that he tries to speak die away upon his lips; for the habit of blasphemy is too strong upon him; he can *blague* upon all the mighty mysteries of heaven and hell, but he *cannot* pray.

Paul Marchmont could not fashion a prayer. Horrible witticisms arose up between him and the words he would have spoken—ghastly *bon mots*, that had seemed so brilliant at a lamp-lit dinner-table, spoken to a joyous accompaniment of champagne-corks and laughter. Ah, me! the world was behind this man now, with all its pleasures; and he looked back upon it, and thought that, even when it seemed gayest and brightest, it was only like a great roaring fair, with flaring lights, and noisy showmen clamoring for ever to a struggling crowd.

How should he die? Should he go upstairs and cut his throat?

He stood before one of his pictures—a pet picture; a girl's face by Millais, looking through the moonlight, fantastically beautiful. He stood before this picture, and he felt one small separate pang amid all his misery as he remembered that Edward and Mary Arundel were now possessors of this particular gem.

"They sha'n't have it," he muttered to himself; "they sha'n't have *this*, at any rate."

He took a penknife from his pocket, and hacked and ripped the canvas savagely, till it hung in ribbons from the deep gilded frame.

Then he smiled to himself, for the first time since he had entered that house, and his eyes flashed with a sudden light.

"I have lived like Sardanapalus for the last year," he cried aloud; "and I will die like Sardanapalus!"

There was a fragile piece of furniture near him,—an *étagère* of marqueterie work, loaded with costly *bric à brac*, Oriental porcelain, Sèvres and Dresden, old Chelsea and crown Derby cups and saucers, and quaint teapots, crawling vermin in Pallissy ware, Indian monstrosities, and all manner of expensive absurdities, heaped together in artistic confusion. Paul Marchmont struck the slim leg of the *étagère* with his foot, and laughed aloud as the fragile toys fell into a ruined heap upon the carpet. He stamped upon the broken china; and the frail cups and saucers crackled like eggshells under his savage feet.

"I will die like Sardanapalus!" he cried; "the King Arbaces shall never rest in the palace I have beautified.

'Now order here
Fagots, pine-nuts, and wither'd leaves, and such
Things as catch fire with one sole spark;
Bring cedar, too, and precious drugs, and spices,
And mighty planks, to nourish a tall pile;
Bring frankincense and myrrh, too; for it is
For a great sacrifice I build the pyre.'

I don't think much of your blank verse, George Gordon Noel Byron. Your lines end on lame syllables; your ten-syllable blank verse lacks the fiery ring of your rhymes. I wonder whether Marchmont Towers is insured? Yes, I remember paying a premium last Christmas. They may have a sharp tussle with the insurance companies though. Yes, I will die like Sardanapalus—no, not like him, for I have no Myrrha to mount the pile and cling about me to the last. Pshaw! a modern Myrrha would leave Sardanapalus to perish alone, and be off to make herself safe with the new king."

Paul snatched up the candle, and went out into the hall. He laughed discordantly, and spoke in loud ringing tones. His manner had that feverish excitement which the French call exaltation. He ran up the broad stairs leading to the long corridor, out of which his own rooms, and his mother's and sister's rooms, opened.

Ah, how pretty they were! How elegant he had made them in his reckless disregard of expense, his artistic delight in the task of beautification! There were no shutters here, and the summer breeze blew in through the broken windows, and stirred the gauzy muslin curtains, the gay chintz draperies, the cloudlike festoons of silk and lace. Paul Marchmont went from room to room with the flaring candle in his hand; and wherever there were curtains or draperies about the windows, the beds, the dressing-tables, the low lounging-chairs, and cosy little sofas, he set alight to them. He did this with wonderful rapidity, leaving flames behind him as he traversed the long corridor, and coming back thus to the stairs. He went downstairs again, and returned to the western drawing-room. Then he blew out his candle, turned out the gas, and waited.

"How soon will it come?" he thought.

The shutters were shut, and the room was quite dark.

"Shall I ever have courage to stop till it comes?"

Paul Marchmont groped his way to the door, double-locked it, and then took the key from the lock.

He went to one of the windows, clambered upon a chair, opened the top shutter, and flung the key out through the broken window. He heard it strike jingling upon the stone terrace and then bound away, Heaven knows where.

"I shan't be able to go out by the door, at any rate," he thought.

It was quite dark in the room, but the reflection of the spreading flames was growing crimson in the sky outside. Mr. Marchmont went away from the window, feeling his way amongst the chairs and tables. He could see the red light through the crevices of the shutters, and a lurid patch of sky through that one window, the upper half of which he had left open. He sat down, somewhere near the centre of the room, and waited.

"The smoke will kill me," he thought. "I shall know nothing of the fire."

He sat quite still. He had trembled violently while he had gone from room to room doing his horrible work; but his nerves seemed steadier now. Steadier! why, he was transformed to stone! His heart seemed to have stopped beating; and he only knew by a sick anguish, a dull aching pain, that it was still in his breast.

He sat waiting and thinking. In that time all the long story of the past was acted before him, and he saw what a wretch he had been. I do not know whether this was penitence; but looking at that enacted story, Paul Marchmont thought that his own part in the play was a mistake, and that it was a foolish thing to be a villain.

* * * * *

When a great flock of frightened people, with a fire-engine out of order, and drawn by whooping men and boys, came hurrying up to the Towers, they found a blazing edifice, which looked like an enchanted castle—great stone-framed windows vomiting flame; tall chimneys toppling down upon a fiery roof; molten lead, like water turned to fire, streaming in flaming cataracts upon the terrace; and all the sky lit up by that vast pile of blazing ruin. Only salamanders, or poor Mr. Braidwood's own chosen band, could have approached Marchmont Towers that night. The Kemberling firemen and the Swampington firemen, who came by-and-by, were neither salamanders nor Braidwoods. They stood aloof and squirted water at the flames, and recoiled aghast by-and-by when the roof came down like an avalanche of blazing timber, leaving only a gaunt gigantic skeleton of red-hot stone where Marchmont Towers once had been.

When it was safe to venture in amongst the ruins—and this was not for many hours after the fire had burnt itself out—people looked for Paul Marchmont; but amidst all that vast chaos of smouldering ashes, there was nothing found that could be identified as the remains of a human being. No one knew where the artist had been at the time of the fire, or indeed whether he had been in the house at all; and the popular opinion was, that Paul had set fire to the mansion, and had fled away before the flames began to spread.

But Lavinia Weston knew better than this. She knew now why her brother had sent her every scrap of valuable property belonging to him. She understood now why he had come back to her to bid her good-night for the second time, and press his cold lips to hers.

CHAPTER THE LAST.

Mary and Edward Arundel saw the awful light in the sky, and heard the voices of the people shouting in the street below, and calling to one another that Marchmont Towers was on fire.

The young mistress of the burning pile had very little concern for her property. She only kept saying, again and again, "O Edward! I hope there is no one in the house. God grant there may be no one in the house!"

And when the flames were highest, and it seemed by the light in the sky as if all Lincolnshire had been blazing, Edward Arundel's wife flung herself upon her knees, and prayed aloud for any unhappy creature that might be in peril.

Oh, if we could dare to think that this innocent girl's prayer was heard before the throne of an Awful Judge, pleading for the soul of a wicked man!

Early the next morning Mrs. Arundel came from Lawford Grange with her confidential maid, and carried off her daughter-in-law and the baby, on the first stage of the journey into Devonshire. Before she left Kemberling, Mary was told that no dead body had been found amongst the ruins of the Towers; and this assertion deluded her into the belief that no unhappy creature had perished. So she went to Dangerfield happier than she had ever been since the sunny days of her honeymoon, to wait there for the coming of Edward Arundel, who was to stay behind to see Richard Paulette and Mr. Gormby, and to secure the testimony of Mr. Weston and Betsy Murrel with a view to the identification of Mary's little son, who had been neither registered nor christened.

I have no need to dwell upon this process of identification, registration, and christening, through which Master Edward Arundel had to pass in the course of the next month. I had rather skip this dry-as-dust business, and go on to that happy time which Edward and his young wife spent together under the oaks at Dangerfield—that bright second honeymoon season, while they were as yet houseless; for a pretty villa-like mansion was being built on the Marchmont property, far away from the dank wood and the dismal river, in a pretty pastoral little nook, which was a fair oasis amidst the general dreariness of Lincolnshire.

I need scarcely say that the grand feature of this happy time was THE BABY. It will be of course easily understood that this child stood alone amongst babies. There never had been another such infant; it was more than probable there would never again be such a one. In every attribute of babyhood he was a twelvemonth in advance of the rest of his race. Prospective greatness was stamped upon his brow. He would be a Clive or a Wellington, unless indeed he should have a fancy for the Bar and the Woolsack, in which case he would be a little more erudite than Lyndhurst, a trifle more eloquent than Brougham. All this was palpable to the meanest capacity in the very manner in which this child crowed in his nurse's arms, or choked himself with farinaceous food, or smiled recognition at his young father, or performed the simplest act common to infancy.

I think Mr. Sant would have been pleased to paint one of those summer scenes at Dangerfield—the proud soldier-father; the pale young wife; the handsome, matronly grandmother; and, as the mystic centre of that magic circle, the toddling flaxen-haired baby, held up by his father's hands, and taking caricature strides in imitation of papa's big steps.

To my mind, it is a great pity that children are not children for ever—that the pretty baby-boy by Sant, all rosy and flaxen and blue-eyed, should ever grow into a great angular pre-Raphaelite hobadahoy, horribly big and out of drawing. But neither Edward nor Mary nor, above all, Mrs. Arundel were of this opinion. They were as eager for the child to grow up and enter for the great races of this life, as some speculative turf magnate who has given a fancy price for a yearling, and is pining to see the animal a far-famed three-year-old, and winner of the double event.

Before the child had cut a double-tooth Mrs. Arundel senior had decided in favour of Eton as opposed to Harrow, and was balancing the conflicting advantages of classical Oxford and mathematical Cambridge; while Edward could not see the baby-boy rolling on the grass, with blue ribbons and sashes fluttering in the breeze, without thinking of his son's future appearance in the uniform of his own regiment, gorgeous in the splendid crush of a levee at St. James's.

How many airy castles were erected in that happy time, with the baby for the foundation-stone of all of them! *The* BABY! Why, that definite article alone expresses an infinity of foolish love and admiration. Nobody says *the* father, the husband, the mother; it is "my" father, my husband, as the case may be. But every baby, from St. Giles's to Belgravia, from Tyburnia to St. Luke's, is "the" baby. The infant's reign is short, but his royalty is supreme, and no one presumes to question his despotic rule.

Edward Arundel almost worshipped the little child whose feeble cry he had heard in the October twilight, and had *not* recognised. He was never tired of reproaching himself for this omission. That baby-voice *ought* to have awakened a strange thrill in the young father's breast.

That time at Dangerfield was the happiest period of Mary's life. All her sorrows had melted away. They did not tell her of Paul Marchmont's suspected fate; they only told her that her enemy had disappeared, and that no one knew whither he had gone. Mary asked once, and once only, about her stepmother; and she was told that Olivia was at Swampington Rectory, living with her father, and that people said she was mad. George Weston had emigrated to Australia, with his wife, and his wife's mother and sister. There had been no prosecution for conspiracy; the disappearance of the principal criminal had rendered that unnecessary.

This was all that Mary ever heard of her persecutors. She did not wish to hear of them; she had forgiven them long ago. I think that in the inner depths of her innocent heart she had forgiven them from the moment she had fallen on her husband's breast in Hester's parlour at Kemberling, and had felt his strong arms clasped about her, sheltering her from all harm for evermore.

She was very happy; and her nature, always gentle, seemed sublimated by the sufferings she had endured, and already akin to that of the angels. Alas, this was Edward Arundel's chief sorrow! This young wife, so precious to him in her fading loveliness, was slipping away from him, even in the hour when they were happiest together—was separated from him even when they were most united. She was separated from him by that unconquerable sadness in his heart, which was prophetic of a great sorrow to come.

Sometimes, when Mary saw her husband looking at her with a mournful tenderness, an almost despairing love in his eyes, she would throw herself into his arms, and say to him:

"You must remember how happy I have been, Edward. O my darling! promise me always to remember how happy I have been."

When the first chill breezes of autumn blew among the Dangerfield oaks, Edward Arundel took his wife southwards, with his mother and the inevitable baby in her train. They went to Nice, and they were very quiet, very happy, in the pretty southern town, with snow-clad mountains behind them, and the purple Mediterranean before.

The villa was building all this time in Lincolnshire. Edward's agent sent him plans and sketches for Mrs. Arundel's approval; and every evening there was some fresh talk about the arrangement of the rooms, and the laying-out of gardens. Mary was always pleased to see the plans and drawings, and to discuss the progress of the work with her husband. She would talk of the billiard-room, and the cosy little smoking-room, and the nurseries for the baby, which were to have a southern aspect, and every advantage calculated to assist the development of that rare and marvellous blossom; and she would plan the comfortable apartments that were to be specially kept for dear grandmamma, who would of course spend a great deal of her time at the Sycamores—the new place was to be called the Sycamores. But Edward could never get his wife to talk of a certain boudoir opening into a tiny conservatory, which he himself had added on to the original architect's plan. He could never get Mary to speak of this particular chamber; and once, when he asked her some question about the colour of the draperies, she said to him, very gently,—

"I would rather you would not think of that room, darling."

"Why, my pet?"

"Because it will make you sorry afterwards."

"Mary, my darling——"

"O Edward! you know,—you must know, dearest,—that I shall never see that place?"

But her husband took her in his arms, and declared that this was only a morbid fancy, and that she was getting better and stronger every day, and would live to see her grandchildren playing under the maples that sheltered the northern side of the new villa. Edward told his wife this, and he believed in the truth of what he said. He could not believe that he was to lose this young wife, restored to him after so many trials. Mary did not contradict him just then; but that night, when he was sitting in her room reading by the light of a shaded lamp after she had gone to bed,—Mary went to bed very early, by order of the doctors, and indeed lived altogether according to medical *régime*, —she called her husband to her.

"I want to speak to you, dear," she said; "there is something that I must say to you."

The young man knelt down by his wife's bed.

"What is it, darling?" he asked.

"You know what we said to-day, Edward?"

"What, darling? We say so many things every day—we are so happy together, and have so much to talk about."

"But you remember, Edward,—you remember what I said about never seeing the Sycamores? Ah! don't stop me, dear love," Mary said reproachfully, for Edward put his lips to hers to stay the current of mournful words,—"don't stop me, dear, for I must speak to you. I want you to know that *it must be*, Edward darling. I want you to remember how happy I have been, and how willing I am to part with you, dear, since it is God's will that we should be parted. And there is something else that I want to say, Edward. Grandmamma told me something—all about Belinda. I want you to promise me that Belinda shall be happy by-and-by; for she has suffered so much, poor girl! And you will love her, and she will love the baby. But you won't love her quite the same way that you loved me, will you, dear? because you never knew her when she was a little child, and very poor. She has never been an orphan, and quite lonely, as I have been. You have never been *all the world* to her."

* * * * *

The Sycamores was finished by the following midsummer, but no one took possession of the newly-built house; no brisk upholsterer's men came, with three-foot rules and pencils and memorandum-books, to take measurements of windows and floors; no wagons of splendid furniture made havoc of the gravel-drive before the principal entrance. The only person who came to the new house was a snuff-taking crone from Stanfield, who brought a turn-up bedstead, a Dutch clock, and a few minor articles of furniture, and encamped in a corner of the best bedroom.

Edward Arundel, senior, was away in India, fighting under Napier and Outram; and Edward Arundel, junior, was at Dangerfield, under the charge of his grandmother.

Perhaps the most beautiful monument in one of the English cemeteries at Nice is that tall white marble cross and kneeling figure, before which strangers pause to read an inscription to the memory of Mary, the beloved wife of Edward Dangerfield Arundel.

THE EPILOGUE.

Four years after the completion of that pretty stuccoed villa, which seemed destined never to be inhabited, Belinda Lawford walked alone up and down the sheltered shrubbery-walk in the Grange garden in the fading September daylight.

Miss Lawford was taller and more womanly-looking than she had been on the day of her interrupted wedding. The vivid bloom had left her cheeks; but I think she was all the prettier because of that delicate pallor, which gave a pensive cast to her countenance. She was very grave and gentle and good; but she had never forgotten the shock of that broken bridal ceremonial in Hillingsworth Church.

The Major had taken his eldest daughter abroad almost immediately after that July day; and Belinda and her father had travelled together very peacefully, exploring quiet Belgian cities, looking at celebrated altar-pieces in dusky cathedrals, and wandering round battle-fields, which the intermingled blood of rival nations had once made one crimson swamp. They had been nearly a twelvemonth absent, and then Belinda returned to assist at the marriage of a younger sister, and to hear that Edward Arundel's wife had died of a lingering pulmonary complaint at Nice.

She was told this: and she was told how Olivia Marchmont still lived with her father at Swampington, and how day by day she went the same round from cottage to cottage, visiting the sick; teaching little children, or sometimes rough-bearded men, to read and write and cipher; reading to old decrepid pensioners; listening to long histories of sickness and trial, and exhibiting an unwearying patience that was akin to sublimity. Passion had burnt itself out in this woman's breast, and there was nothing in her mind now but remorse, and the desire to perform a long penance, by reason of which she might in the end be forgiven.

But Mrs. Marchmont never visited anyone alone. Wherever she went, Barbara Simmons accompanied her, constant as her shadow. The Swampington people said this was because the Rector's daughter was not quite right in her mind; and there were times when she forgot where she was, and would have wandered away in a purposeless manner, Heaven knows where, had she not been accompanied by her faithful servant. Clever as the Swampington people and the Kemberling people might be in finding out the business of their neighbours, they never knew that Olivia Marchmont had been consentient to the hiding-away of her stepdaughter. They looked upon her, indeed, with considerable respect, as a heroine by whose exertions Paul Marchmont's villany had been discovered. In the hurry and confusion of the scene at Hillingsworth Church, nobody had taken heed of Olivia's incoherent self-accusations: Hubert Arundel was therefore spared the misery of knowing the extent of his daughter's sin.

Belinda Lawford came home in order to be present at her sister's wedding; and the old life began again for her, with all the old duties that had once been so pleasant. She went about them very cheerfully now. She worked for her poor pensioners, and took the chief burden of the housekeeping off her mother's hands. But though she jingled her keys with a cheery music as she went about the house, and though she often sang to herself over her work, the old happy smile rarely lit up her face. She went about her duties rather like some widowed matron who had lived her life, than a girl before whom the future lies, mysterious and unknown.

It has been said that happiness comes to the sleeper—the meaning of which proverb I take to be, that Joy generally comes to us when we least look for her lovely face. And it was on this September afternoon, when Belinda loitered in the garden after her round of small duties was finished, and she was free to think or dream at her leisure, that happiness came to her,—unexpected, unhoped-for, supreme; for, turning at one end of the sheltered alley, she saw Edward Arundel standing at the other end, with his hat in his hand, and the summer wind blowing amongst his hair.

Miss Lawford stopped quite still. The old-fashioned garden reeled before her eyes, and the hard-gravelled path seemed to become a quaking bog. She could not move; she stood still, and waited while Edward came towards her.

"Letitia has told me about you, Linda," he said; "she has told me how true and noble you have been; and she sent me here to look for a wife, to make new sunshine in my empty home,—a young mother to smile upon my motherless boy."

Edward and Belinda walked up and down the sheltered alley for a long time, talking a great deal of the sad past, a little of the fair-seeming future. It was growing dusk before they went in at the old-fashioned half-glass door leading into the drawing-room, where Mrs. Lawford and her younger daughters were sitting, and where Lydia, who was next to Belinda, and had been three years married to the Curate of Hillingsworth, was nursing her second baby.

"Has she said 'yes'?" this young matron cried directly; for she had been told of Edward's errand to the Grange. "But of course she has. What else should she say, after refusing all manner of people, and giving herself the airs of an old-maid? Yes, um pressus Pops, um Aunty Lindy's going to be marriedypariedy," concluded the Curate's wife, addressing her three-months-old baby in that peculiar patois which is supposed to be intelligible to infants by reason of being unintelligible to everybody else.

"I suppose you are not aware that my future brother-in-law is a major?" said Belinda's third sister, who had been struggling with a variation by Thalberg, all octaves and accidentals, and who twisted herself round upon her music-stool to address her sister. "I suppose you are not aware that you have been talking to Major Arundel, who has done all manner of splendid things in the Punjaub? Papa told us all about it five minutes ago."

It was as much as Belinda could do to support the clamorous felicitations of her sisters, especially the unmarried damsels, who were eager to exhibit themselves in the capacity of bridesmaids; but by-and-by, after dinner, the Curate's wife drew her sisters away from that shadowy window in which Edward Arundel and Belinda were sitting, and the lovers were left to themselves.

That evening was very peaceful, very happy, and there were many other evenings like it before Edward and Belinda completed that ceremonial which they had left unfinished more than five years before.

The Sycamores was very prettily furnished, under Belinda's superintendence; and as Reginald Arundel had lately married, Edward's mother came to live with her younger son, and brought with her the idolised grandchild, who was now a tall, yellow-haired boy of six years old.

There was only one room in the Sycamores which was never tenanted by any one of that little household except Edward himself, who kept the key of the little chamber in his writing-desk, and only allowed the servants to go in at stated intervals to keep everything bright and orderly in the apartment.

The shut-up chamber was the boudoir which Edward Arundel had planned for his first wife. He had ordered it to be furnished with the very furniture which he had intended for Mary. The rosebuds and butterflies on the walls, the guipure curtains lined with pale blush-rose silk, the few chosen books in the little cabinet near the fireplace, the Dresden breakfast-service, the statuettes and pictures, were things he had fixed upon long ago in his own mind as the decorations for his wife's apartment. He went into the room now and then, and looked at his first wife's picture—a crayon sketch taken in London before Mary and her husband started for the South of France. He looked a little wistfully at this picture, even when he was happiest in the new ties that bound him to life, and all that is brightest in life.

Major Arundel took his eldest son into this room one day, when young Edward was eight or nine years old, and showed the boy his mother's portrait.

"When you are a man, this place will be yours, Edward," the father said. "*You* can give your wife this room, although I have never given it to mine. You will tell her that it was built for your mother, and that it was built for her by a husband who, even when most grateful to God for every new blessing he enjoyed, never ceased to be sorry for the loss of his first love."

And so I leave my soldier-hero, to repose upon laurels that have been hardly won, and secure in that modified happiness which is chastened by the memory of sorrow. I leave him with bright children crowding round his knees, a loving wife smiling at him across those fair childish heads. I leave him happy and good and useful, filling his place in the world, and bringing up his children to be wise and virtuous men and women in the days that are to come. I leave him, above all, with the serene lamp of faith for ever burning in his soul, lighting the image of that other world in which there is neither marrying nor giving in marriage, and where his dead wife will smile upon him from amidst the vast throng of angel faces—a child for ever and ever before the throne of God!

THE END.